BETWEEN WORLDS 5

HIDE AND SEEK

LORI WOLF-HEFFNER

HEAD IN THE GROUND PUBLISHING

ISBN 978-1-989465-08-0 (Paperback Edition)

ISBN 978-1-989465-09-7 (Ebook Edition)

ISBN 978-1-989465-10-3 (Large Print Edition)

Some characters and events in this book are fictitious. Any similarity to real persons, living or dead, is coincidental and not intended by the author.

Editing by Susan Fish

Cover design by Fresh Design

All photographs from Shutterstock

Head in the Ground Publishing

Waterloo, Ontario, Canada

headintheground.com

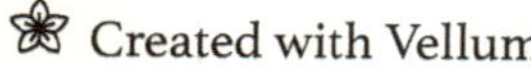 Created with Vellum

Dedicated to my Opa, John Heffner, Sr., who celebrated his 90th birthday a month before this book was published. His dream led him to Canada, where he has touched thousands of lives through his business and community involvement over the decades.

CHAPTER ONE

uliana's phone buzzed and she checked the message.

Call me when you have a sec.

"Who's that?" Mom asked as she draped Juliana's costume bag over the back of a kitchen chair. They had just returned home to Kitchener from Juliana's first competition with her new dance studio.

"Um, just Rachel," Juliana said. Her stomach twisted. Because she had been in only four dances this competition instead of her usual ten or twelve, Juliana and Mom had had lots of time to hang out. After all that had happened this month, Juliana had really needed and enjoyed the time with her mother. Why had her aunt put her in a position where she had to lie to Mom?

"How's she doing?" Mom asked.

Why did I say Rachel? Juliana asked herself. Her best friend's mom had been killed by a drunk driver a few weeks before. It would have been better if she'd said it was Jasmine, her new friend from dance, or Meghan, a friend from school.

"She's, uh, you know, sad and all that stuff." *All that stuff? Can I be any ruder?* she asked herself.

Juliana set her dance bag on to the floor and excused herself. As she stood in the washroom, she texted.

Just got back. Will call later about your plans. Mom's suspicious.

In response, she got a thumbs-up emoji.

Juliana heard Mom carrying luggage to her room—the walls and doors in this old bungalow were paper thin. She flushed the toilet, washed her hands so they'd smell like soap, and came back to the kitchen.

"Anything else I can get from the car?" she asked Mom.

"One more bag, if you wouldn't mind? I'll make us something to eat."

Although the competition had been in Toronto, only an hour's drive away, all the dancers and their parents had spent the two nights in a hotel to save on driving. Juliana had loved it—she was finally beginning to feel like part of the team.

Juliana headed out into the winter air, her breath visible each time she exhaled. She thought about how she and Mom had talked during long breaks between dances.

They had talked about Mom's days in dance and how she had preferred ballet. Juliana liked tap better: you could do it anywhere, wearing anything, and even if you were dead tired but had the urge to dance, you could still shuffle your feet to a rhythm inside your head. They had also talked about the move from Calgary halfway across the country to Kitchener and how Mom and Dad hadn't expected Juliana to experience so many difficulties. Juliana had even let herself cry in front of Mom one night as she rambled off everything: that she missed her friends, that she and Rachel were maybe best friends no longer, that despite her best efforts her average from first semester hadn't even hit eighty percent, when she was aiming for ninety.

"One last bag?" Juliana asked aloud, staring at the last piece of luggage in the trunk. "It's the heaviest one!"

Juliana hoisted the last piece of luggage out of the trunk and pressed the button to close the hatch. Limping to one side to compensate for the suitcase's weight, she opened the screen door at the side of the house and barely made it onto the landing before the old, aluminum-framed door slammed behind her.

She yanked up the suitcase and then set it down on each of the two stairs as she climbed into the kitchen. Mom had some toast, sunflower seed butter, and jam ready on the table.

"You looked amazing on stage, Jules. Opa and Oma would've been so proud of you," Mom said as Juliana made her sandwich. Opa, Mom's father, was away on a seniors' trip to Cuba. "It's too bad Oma ..." Mom's voice trailed off. "It's been eleven years since she died. But this is probably the last time Opa'll be able to go away, so Anne, Peter, and I had to make it happen." Mom sounded sad. "But he'll see you at the next one."

Juliana bit into her sandwich and smiled. "Thanks for this," she said, hoping to lift Mom's mood a bit. She was beginning to understand how hard it must have been for Mom to live with her dad again, and to watch him slowly lose his memory.

"What happened to you?" Mom asked, her mood changing. "You're—don't take this the wrong way—but you're oddly happy."

Juliana feigned an angry look.

"That's better." Mom yawned and looked at her watch. "I'm going to get ready for bed but I'll try to wait up for—"

The door unlocked.

"Dad!" Juliana shouted. She jumped up from her chair and ran to hug her father before he could even get through the door.

"You're going to knock me down!" he said, laughing, and gave her a hug. "Competition was good?"

"Two of our groups got platinum, the third one high gold, and the fourth one gold!"

Dad gave Mom a confused look.

"I know," she said. "I have to look it up all the time, too.

When I was her age, it was gold, silver, and bronze, and that was it. The rest lost. What she's saying is that they did really well."

"That's great," Dad said, settling himself at the table to make himself a sandwich. They talked about Dad's trip and the dance competition for fifteen minutes and then Mom yawned.

"I'm just going to take my shoes downstairs," Juliana said. Mom looked puzzled. Juliana realized she should've kept her mouth shut: she always kept her shoes in her bedroom, especially after she'd forgotten her tap shoes at her first practice with her new studio. "Um, because dance is cancelled tomorrow night so I should practise."

"But we're eating at Anne's tomorrow evening," Mom said. "You've got the night off and Peter's in town for once." Aunt Anne and Uncle Peter were Mom's sister and brother. Aunt Anne was the oldest and Uncle Peter the youngest, which left Mom in the middle. *Like a sandwich*, Juliana realized.

Dad knew what Juliana was trying to do. "Good idea, sweetie," he said to Juliana. "It's always good to prepare ahead of time, but you know that. Uh, sorry I'm going to miss family dinner again, though." He winked secretly at Juliana as he put his arm around Mom's waist. "Katy, you're tired and I just drove from Quebec City today. Let's go to bed. Juliana's too young to go to bed at eight, and we're too old to stay up."

Once Mom turned around to head to their bedroom, Juliana gave Dad a quick smile, which he returned. She carried her dance bag to the basement and dialled Aunt Anne.

"Juliana?"

"Yeah, it's me. I'm in the basement. Dad helped hurry Mom to bed."

"Great. Can we do it two Saturdays from now? I know we'll miss her birthday itself, but everyone's free on my end, including Peter, and it'll be easier to surprise her after her birthday's happened."

"I texted Dad earlier today, and he said it'll work."

"Terrific!"

Juliana sprang into the air, a little jump of joy, though she still didn't enjoy lying to Mom about this: Juliana was helping Aunt Anne plan Mom's surprise birthday party. It wasn't a special-number birthday—Mom was turning forty-four—but it was the first one she would have in town in almost twenty years. Mom had moved out west to Calgary about two years before Juliana was born to accept a job promotion. Aside from the odd visit at Christmas or Easter, Mom had rarely come home.

"So your dad said he can look after ordering the food?" Aunt Anne confirmed.

"Yeah. He said he can order while he's driving since he has no one else to talk to. He's delivering something all the way to...Kenora? I think he said Kenora." Juliana was still getting used to Dad's long-haul routes on this side of the country.

"Great. I'll do the baking: I have Modr's recipes written down." *Modr* was what Mom and her siblings called their mom. They called their father *Tata*.

Lots of people—new and old friends—were being invited. Juliana had her gift planned, but it was a long shot: Opa had told her about an old dance photo of Mom that had really embarrassed her, because Mom had had to dress up like some kind of white, fluffy toy. At first, Juliana had wanted to find it just to see her mom in a kid's costume. *She would've been really cute*, Juliana thought. But now the photo had become more important.

Aunt Anne and Juliana confirmed a few more details, and then Juliana had to ask about the picture.

"Do you remember a photo of Mom in a fluffy, white costume of some kind?"

"The fur bag?" Aunt Anne asked with a chuckle.

Juliana giggled. "Is that what she called it?"

"Oh, yeah," Aunt Anne said. "She hated it. I'm pretty sure she tore that picture up—it disappeared at some point. But it's too bad...it was her first competition that year, and she did really well. Then she got a special role in the year-end show because of it. But all she could think of was how embarrassing the costume was. Why do you ask?"

"When Opa told me about it, I was thinking it'd be a fun gift for Mom—like, an embarrassing-but-fun-gift, and

Opa said it's around here somewhere. But on the weekend, Mom ran into an old dance friend at the competition. Tanya—"

Aunt Anne immediately jumped in. "Tanya O'Connor! No way! She and your mom were good friends when they were young. Wow. Small world, eh?"

"Yeah, I guess so." Why did adults always say it was a small world when they ran into someone they hadn't seen in a long time? "Anyway, she reminded Mom about the picture. Mom told me that she regretted not keeping the photo."

There was a pause, and Juliana assumed Aunt Anne was thinking.

After a moment, Aunt Anne responded. "Wow. But if she didn't tear it up, then I'm certain that photo went missing decades ago. Someone would've found it by now if it still existed. Trust me—my kids did enough snooping in that house when they were young. You may be out of luck."

"But Opa said he was sure it was still here."

Aunt Anne sighed—it was a sigh of regret, though, and not impatience. "You know how his mind works sometimes. He may be thinking of something thirty years ago and not know it."

"I suppose. But still, it might be here." She didn't say, *It has to be here, because I have nothing else to give her that would mean so much to her.*

"Juliana!" Uncle Peter beamed. Juliana wouldn't recognize her uncle without that huge grin. She'd even seen family photos from when Mom and her siblings were kids. He had smiled like that back then, too.

"Hi," Juliana said. Did he know he looked like a nerd? That he had a mullet didn't help.

Uncle Peter put his arm around a man's shoulders. "This is my niece, Katy's only child, Juliana Roth." The man nodded. To Juliana, Uncle Peter said, "And this is my partner, Brian Yamamoto."

"Hi," Juliana repeated.

Brian's smile was gentler and he didn't look like he was high on something. He shook Juliana's hand. "Nice to meet you. Pete said you were at a dance competition this weekend? I used to dance." Brian wiggled his hips and shook his head, making him look like he'd stuck his finger in an electrical socket.

Juliana tried to smile. What was she supposed to say to that? She scanned the room for Sophie, hoping her cousin might save her.

Brian noticed her reaction. "It's okay, you can laugh. Pete laughs at me when we dance at weddings." He playfully punched Uncle Peter in the shoulder.

"I know I make fun of you," Uncle Peter said. "But at

least you got to dance as a kid." He looked at Juliana. "I wasn't allowed to. 'Boys don't dance' and all that."

Boys don't dance? Juliana knew fewer boys danced than girls, but she'd always assumed it was because boys just liked sports and video games more, not because they weren't allowed to dance. *That'd be stupid*, she thought.

"Supper's ready!" Aunt Anne called to everyone.

Relieved that this bizarre introduction had been interrupted, Juliana followed everyone to the dining room. Aunt Anne had six kids, with Scott the youngest at eight and Rebecca the oldest at twenty-three, so Aunt Anne and Uncle Phillip had a large house and the dining room could seat a lot of people.

"Hey, Juliana!" Sophie said, coming out of the kitchen. At twelve, Sophie was the only girl close in age to Juliana in the family. Juliana had recently begun helping Sophie with her math homework, so she knew her the best of all her cousins. "You finally met Brian?"

"Yup."

"Did he try to dance for you?"

"Yup."

Sophie giggled. "He always does that."

The two cousins sat beside each other at the table. The entire family was there, with only Dad and Opa missing. The first time Juliana had faced all these people had been in Opa's tiny kitchen. Juliana had become so overwhelmed that she had sprinted into the basement. But that had been two months ago. Now, she had at least gotten used to the size of her "new" family and knew their names. Sitting with all of them in this large room also helped her feel more comfortable around them.

"Dig in, everyone!" Aunt Anne said.

Mom had her phone at the table, and Juliana wanted to complain that it wasn't fair that adults got to keep their phones out when she didn't. But when Mom announced why she was scrolling through it, Juliana brightened up.

"You guys need to see this video from the weekend," Mom said. "Juliana was amazing."

Everyone waited for a moment, but Mom kept scrolling, her brow furrowing as she searched.

"Sophie, pass the potatoes," Rebecca said in the silence.

Sophie didn't move.

"Sophie?"

Aunt Anne spoke up. "Not here, Rebecca."

"Not ever," Sophie muttered under her breath. Juliana had no idea what she was talking about.

"She has to learn, Mom," Rebecca said.

Aunt Anne gave Rebecca a stern look and Juliana got the distinct impression that only the Morgan family knew what was going on.

"The white bowl in the centre and to your left, Sophie. That's the potatoes," Rebecca said.

Sophie picked up the bowl without looking at it directly and handed it to her sister.

"Did you find the video?" Uncle Peter said in an effort to release the tension at the table.

"No..." Mom said, still scrolling through her phone. "I took something like six hundred photos but only four videos. Give me a sec. You guys really need to see this. Juliana's improved so much this year."

"Really?" Sophie asked. "Wish I could've seen it."

There was another awkward silence. Juliana knew that Sophie's wish had two meanings: she wished she could have been there, and she wished she could have physically seen it. Sophie had begun losing her eyesight a couple of years ago, and so far as Juliana understood, the vision loss began in the middle, the vision you needed to read and to see someone's eyes. Aunt Anne had said once it was like having a really tiny sticker over the middle of each eye: you couldn't see through the stickers, but you could see around them. On a few occasions, Juliana had waved to Sophie from far away as she had walked up to their house, and Sophie hadn't reacted. But when the two talked face-to-face, Juliana wouldn't have known that Sophie had already lost some of her eyesight: she made eye contact with Juliana like a regular seeing person. It was still confusing to Juliana, but she was learning.

"It sounds like you were amazing," Uncle Peter said. "I wish I could've seen it, too." Sophie's face relaxed.

"We actually did really good," Juliana said.

Sophie beamed.

"How's that searching coming, Katy?" Uncle Peter asked.

"You can never find things, can you?" Aunt Anne asked her sister jokingly.

"Because I had to hide my things from you," Mom replied. "Otherwise you'd steal them. Now I think I hide them from myself out of habit."

Everyone laughed.

"You left your things lying around. If I needed it, I didn't see a problem with that," Aunt Anne replied.

Mom looked up. "That was your reasoning? Really?"

Juliana couldn't tell if the joke had turned into an argument now, and judging by the awkwardness that had returned again in the room, neither could anyone else.

"I can't believe that my week off coincided with Tata's trip to Cuba," Uncle Peter said. "But my client didn't need me, so I thought I'd spend it at home."

Mom smiled, though her smile was no competition for Uncle Peter's. "We're glad you could make it. Where's this client?"

"They're headquartered in Kingston, so that's where I've been staying, but they'll soon be sending me to France. I just don't know when yet."

Juliana didn't know what Uncle Peter did for a living except that it had something to do with factories and that it took him away often, for long periods of time, and around the world.

"France is beautiful," Uncle Phillip, Aunt Anne's husband, said. "I did a paid internship there in my twenties."

"I can't wait to go back. How's Tata doing?" Uncle Peter asked, returning the conversation to Opa.

"We haven't heard from him so far so that's probably good," Mom said, "But generally? Not too good." In fact, Opa's declining memory was the main reason the Roths had moved back to Mom's hometown in the first place. Aunt Anne still had four kids in school, and with all the after-school driving, she had found it hard to look after their father, too, even though they only lived a three-minute walk away. The Roths had moved in to keep a better eye on Opa, to help him with his care, and to cook for him.

"*Verdammt*," Uncle Peter said in response to Mom, catching Juliana off guard. He spoke German? She knew Mom and Aunt Anne understood Opa when he spoke German, but she'd never heard them reply in German.

"Oh!" Mom's phone rang and vibrated. She excused herself from the table.

"Great," Juliana said. "She's being called in to work."

"Really?" Uncle Peter asked. "I get the week off and everyone's running off?"

Conversation ground to a halt again, the clinking of cutlery on plates the only sound as people ate. Mom returned.

"I'm sorry," she said. "Manager's gotten sick. Must be

this ridiculous weather. I don't recall the winters being so... I don't know...moody. But I've got to go in and cover for him." She looked at Peter. "Nice to see you again, and sorry I can't hang around more. But Anne can catch you up on what's happening with Tata."

Or I could, Juliana thought, because sometimes it felt like she was the one looking after him. When they had first arrived in Kitchener, she wasn't sure if Opa actually had dementia. But now she saw signs of it almost daily, like forgetfulness and brief outbursts of anger. Opa had even once believed for a few minutes that he was back home, in Semlak, a village in Romania, and that Juliana needed to start finding a husband because she was fourteen.

As everyone said their good-byes to Mom, though, Juliana realized Mom's leaving opened up a golden opportunity for her. Once the front door closed, she asked about the dance photo.

"You still believe it's around somewhere?" Aunt Anne asked. She laughed and shook her head. "Your mother probably threw it out and forgot. She hated that photo. Don't you remember, Peter?"

Uncle Peter laughed. "Oh, man, do I ever." He smiled at Juliana. "She was so angry about it. I think I was...what?... Eight? She terrified me when she got angry."

"But do you know what happened to it?" Juliana asked. "Opa's pretty sure it's in the house somewhere."

Uncle Peter shook his head. "Now that you ask, no, I

have no idea anymore. But I'm pretty sure she wouldn't want to see—"

Juliana interrupted him. "Actually, she does now." She explained what Mom had said about it.

Aunt Anne and Uncle Peter tried to think, and for a moment, Juliana hoped they would remember. But eventually both shook their heads.

"No, I think Annie's right. Your mom hated that costume so much, she must've thrown the photo out. Too bad—sounds like she's regretting something."

"Can you pass the steak?" Juliana's cousin Dean asked.

As the meal continued, Juliana couldn't help but believe Opa that the photo was still in existence. But if no one remembered what had happened to it, then Juliana would have to figure it out the hard way...by searching every nook and cranny of Opa's house herself.

This isn't going to be easy, she thought. *But it'll make the best birthday gift ever if I can find it.*

CHAPTER TWO

With Palm Sunday only a week away, Elisabeth was becoming increasingly nervous. If she studied hard enough, she would pass her confirmation and become a *großmädchen* in the church. In other words, she would no longer be considered a child and was one step closer to being a married woman: you could only begin dancing with boys and eventually marry one after your confirmation. Because confirmands were neither children nor married, during church services, *großmädchen* and *großbuben* (as the confirmed boys were called) sat in rows of pews next to the altar, separate from the children in the balcony and the married and widowed congregants in the nave.

"What if I forget one of the Ten Commandments?" Elisabeth asked.

Maria, Elisabeth's best friend, who was a year older and therefore already confirmed, squeezed Elisabeth's hands. "You need to stop worrying! I passed, and I'm certain I didn't study half as much as you."

Elisabeth laughed. Maria, her mom, and brother had come for a visit after church. As usual, the adults—Mammi and Haibach Anni—sat in the back room, the only formal room of the three rooms in the house. Mammi and Haibach Anni were covered in black from head to toe: a black headscarf tied under the chin hid their hair; a black *tschurak*, a fitted, thin, long-sleeved jacket sitting a few inches over the waist, enveloped their bodices; and a black skirt, supported by layers of white underskirts and covered by a dark blue apron, hid their legs until just above their ankles, which were covered in socks knitted in alternating blue and white horizontal stripes.

The children occupied the front room, where the Schuhmachers entertained close family and slept. Maria's father would come later and join them for lunch since, with Tata away in America, he had no one to talk to at the Schuhmacher household.

Elisabeth, her two sisters, and Maria were all squeezed together on the couch, while eight-year-old Luki and Joschi, Maria's brother, sat under the table, playing with Luki's rubber ball and dried, cut corn cobs.

"Elisabeth hasn't helped me with my knitting," Elisabeth's six-year-old sister, Rosina, complained.

"That's not true!" Elisabeth replied, surprised by the sudden accusation.

"I have to knit by myself a lot."

"Because I have to look after other chores!"

Maria laughed, and Rosina looked indignant. "I brought my knitting along," Maria said. "I can knit with you after lunch, if you'd like."

"No."

"See what I have to deal with?" Elisabeth asked Maria. "She wants something and then she doesn't." Maria smiled.

"Well, I have to help more around the house," Anna said. Almost ten now, she was no longer a little girl, but she didn't want to grow up either, making her a pitchfork in Elisabeth's side sometimes.

"You have to help more?" Elisabeth said. "I have to manage the whole household. You wouldn't last a day in my shoes."

"But I still have to go to school," Anna countered.

"All of us have to help our families," Maria said gently. "Your sister does a lot for all three of you."

Anna crossed her arms and knit her eyebrows together. "So do I. But I'm smart in school because I do my homework. That's what Herr Blum tells me. That's why he always has me sit at the front."

"We still have chores to do," Elisabeth said. "Even when I went to school, I had to do my chores." Elisabeth had finished school two years before, after grade six, like all other German Lutheran children in Semlak. Tata had continued to teach Elisabeth what he could, using the family's encyclopedia set, which had been handed down from his father. Spending that time with Tata learning about the world was what Elisabeth missed most with her father being away.

Maria interrupted the argument and Elisabeth's thoughts by offering a diversion: a relative had sent her a magazine from America. Elisabeth had already seen it but was eager to see it again.

"Now, let me turn the pages," Maria said to the younger sisters, "or I won't let you look." With the mischievous smile Elisabeth knew only too well, Maria opened the cover slower than a snail crawls. Elisabeth's sisters jumped up and down in anticipation.

"You sound like a gaggle of geese over there!" Mammi shouted through the kitchen to the front room. The comment was not a compliment.

Anna and Rosina attempted to muffle their giggling. After Maria opened up the magazine, the girls gasped at the beautiful dresses, elegant hairstyles, and glamorous poses. Wondering what all the commotion was about, Luki stopped playing with Joschi.

"*Ew...*" he said. "Those women look ugly."

Rosina glared at her brother. "Those dresses aren't for you: you're a boy!"

"Be quiet!" Mammi scolded from the back room. "We can hardly have a reasonable conversation in here."

Haibach Anni turned her head to look out the door, too. "Ah, Maria's magazine. She pages through it every day."

"A waste of time," Mammi declared.

"Yes, but my mother's cousin sent it to her. I can't tell her to ignore a gift."

Mammi disagreed, saying that maybe America was making this relative forget the importance of hard work. She offered Haibach Anni more tea and they returned to their own conversation.

Maria pointed at a page with a drawing on it. "Aren't they elegant?" she asked.

Rosina tore the magazine out of Maria's hands and ran it over to Mammi.

"Rosina!" Elisabeth said, but her sister ignored her.

"Look at these shoes!" Rosina said, her voice filled with wonder. "They're eggelant!"

Elisabeth didn't know whether to admonish her sister again or smile at her mistake.

Everyone else in the front room followed Rosina through the kitchen to the back room to see Mammi and Haibach Anni's reactions. Rosina held the magazine open to a drawing of a woman with short hair, a lovely, wide-brimmed hat, a light jacket that reached as far down as a *tschurak* but hung straight, a skirt that waved in the wind and reached down to half-way between the knees and ankles, and then a simple but elegant pair of shoes that had a heel and pointed toes but no straps or laces.

"You'd sink into the mud in those," Mammi said.

"But they're not for work, Lissa," Haibach Anni replied. "They're for special occasions, like church, dances, and weddings. They are very elegant indeed."

Mammi drew her lips into a tight line that said she still disagreed. She had taken over Tata's shoemaking business in his absence. She could make dress slippers out of satin and everyday slippers and ankle-high boots out of leather for women; slippers, shoes, and tall boots out of leather for men; and ankle-high boots out of leather for children. That was it.

"I could maybe embroider a nice decoration for them," Anna said. Although she often pouted and whined to Elisabeth, she acted like a polite little girl to other adults, including Mammi.

Rosina piped up. "I could knit a square for each one."

"A square?" Elisabeth placed her hands on her hips. "Where would we put a square on a shoe?"

"Mammi's the shoemaker," Rosina stated. "She can decide."

"Enough," Mammi said. "We do not live in America. We live here. Our people have traditions, they like simple shoes and boots. They are easy to polish and repair." She looked again at the drawing. "Besides, our shoes don't make deep holes in our floors that will be hard to fix on Saturday."

Every Saturday, all the women and girls in every German household got down on their hands and knees and scrubbed the home from top to bottom. That included dampening the mud-and-chaff floors and then smoothing out any divots and holes in them. The back-room floor didn't need as much scrubbing because it had a rug in the middle, but that required regular washing.

"Besides," Elisabeth added, "planting season starts soon. We have our farmland to work, and this year Anna will be helping me with the kitchen garden." She turned to her sister. "You won't have time to help Mammi with new shoes."

Anna scowled at Elisabeth.

"Put it away," Mammi commanded, pointing at the magazine. "It's filling your minds with too many useless ideas."

The girls protested, though, and even Haibach Anni encouraged Mammi to leave them to their harmless pursuits.

"I agree with Mammi," Luki added. "These shoes are useless. I like the shoes Mammi makes."

Luki had been helping Mammi in the workshop most days after school, ever since Tata had left in November. As a boy, there was very little in the house Luki had to help with, but he was expected to learn his father's trade.

Anna swatted Luki on the back of the head. "They're elegant and beautiful," she declared. Luki pulled at the braid that sat flat and centred up the back of Anna's head. Anna screamed and pressed down with one hand on the comb that held it in place while trying to grab Luki's own hair. Mammi jumped up from her chair, her face turning red. Elisabeth knew she would hit them so she tried to wedge herself between her brother and sister.

Jesus, why can't You make them behave? she prayed.

A KNOCK AT THE KITCHEN DOOR SIGNALLED THAT MARIA'S father had arrived. Elisabeth opened it and welcomed him in. Haibach Adam handed Elisabeth his hat and outer jacket, which she carried to the back room to hang up in one of the wardrobes. The weather outside was finally warming up. The snow had all but melted, so on dry days, no one had to remove their shoes before coming in the house.

"How is Lukas?" he asked her, referring to Tata.

"He's doing well," she answered. "The postcard he sent along with the magazine to Maria was a very nice surprise."

He nodded. "I thought so, too, when I saw it."

She led him into the back room, where the others were already sitting around the dinner table. Maria and Joschi smiled, and Mammi nodded her hello. "Now that you're here," Mammi said, "we can serve lunch. Lissika?"

Elisabeth knew what that meant: Mammi would sit while the children brought in the food. Elisabeth was happy to help. Mammi was expecting a baby, and the midwife had said several weeks ago that Mammi needed to rest every day: Mammi had been getting thinner for some time because she hadn't been able to keep food down. Elisabeth was glad to serve if it helped Mammi take care of the baby inside her.

"I'll put this away," Maria said, referring to the magazine the children had opened again. "And then I can help you."

Maria had helped Elisabeth often over the past few months, including bringing over soup when the family had caught the Spanish flu. It had taken the lives of several from their congregation but had spared the Schuhmachers. Maria also knew how to lift Elisabeth's spirits, and Elisabeth could tell her almost anything, so long as she didn't mind it being passed around the congregation. Maria often forgot if a friend asked her not to share something with others.

Maria slid the magazine into her satchel by the kitchen door and closed the cover.

"And how's the man of the house?" Haibach Adam asked Luki.

Luki stuck out his chest, lifted his chin, reached out his hand and answered, "Fine, thank you."

Haibach Adam shook Luki's hand. "A nice, firm grasp there, Luki. Your father taught you that, didn't he?"

No, Elisabeth thought. *I showed him that.*

But Luki nodded with pride and then turned to Mammi and announced he was going to check on the cows and horses in the barn.

"You've done that twice today already," Mammi said. "It can wait."

Luki lifted his chin more. "I'm the man of the house," he declared. "It's my duty."

Elisabeth lifted her eyebrows, and Maria, who'd returned from the kitchen, attempted to stifle a giggle. Luki marched out of the back room, and soon Anna followed.

"I have to go," she said, meaning she needed to use the outhouse, located behind the animal stalls.

Elisabeth turned to Rosina to help with carrying food to the dinner table, but Rosina had moved to the front room, where it was quieter and warmer, and had started knitting her scarf. When Elisabeth called into the front room, Rosina insisted she had to keep knitting: she was still only on her fifth row.

"Rosina," Mammi called through the house, her voice firm. "You'll kneel in corn if you do not listen to your sister."

Rosina's mouth turned upside down, but she stood up,

stomped with one foot on the ground, and set her knitting on the table.

"If you do that one more time, you will also get the belt," Mammi threatened.

Elisabeth shuddered. She didn't have the Bible memorized, but she was certain nowhere did it say that Jesus hit children.

"What do you say?" Mammi asked, a threatening tone in her voice.

"I'm sorry," Rosina said meekly.

"Now go and bring in the bread, and listen to your sister."

When Rosina did as she was told, Haibach Anni and Haibach Adam nodded in approval.

Rosina's immediate obedience was a blessing, to be sure, but Elisabeth wondered if physically punishing a child followed in Jesus's footsteps. Hadn't Martin Luther said that it was important to follow exactly what Jesus had said in the Bible? That was why the Catholic Pope hadn't liked Martin Luther.

"You really should consider it, Lissa," Haibach Anni said to Mammi at the door. "If you can make shoes like the ones in that magazine, I'm certain you won't have to worry about money while Lukas is away. I know several ladies who would buy them in a heartbeat."

Elisabeth nodded her agreement, Rosina again offered to knit squares for them, and Anna suggested she could embroider them—especially the satin shoes.

"You'll be busy with household chores and gardening," Elisabeth reminded her sister. Anna shot her a look, not wanting to make another scene in front of the guests.

"No," Mammi said firmly. "Our people do not need fancy shoes. They need ones that do what shoes are meant to do: protect your feet and make you look respectable. The shoes my husband and I make do just that."

"I think so, too!" Luki said.

Haibach Anni shrugged her shoulders. "Very well. If you should change your mind, let me know: I'd be your first customer."

Everyone gave one another kisses and hugs, and Haibach Adam shook Luki's hand. "You keep looking after your family," he said. Luki nodded.

Maria gave Elisabeth another kiss on the cheek and was the first out the door. Joschi followed her, and the two raced to the street.

"Maria!" her mother called out. "Act like a lady!"

Her father shook his head at the satchel still lying on the floor. "She always forgets things," he said.

"Anna's the same," Elisabeth said. Her sister shot her another look.

Haibach Adam picked up the satchel, and the Haibachs walked home.

It was mid-afternoon. With her siblings outside playing with friends and Mammi lying down for a nap, Elisabeth took the opportunity to study. Palm Sunday was next week, and Elisabeth still had to memorize several passages from Luther's *Small Catechism*, passages explaining several important aspects of Christian faith.

A knock at the door interrupted her, so she hurried to answer it before it awoke Mammi.

To her surprise, it was Maria. Not wanting Maria to see Mammi sleeping lest Maria tell others, who would then think Mammi was lazy, Elisabeth joined Maria outside under the overhang that ran along the side of the house.

"I'm sorry to disturb you," Maria began, and Elisabeth assured her she was always happy to see her friend. Looking a little relieved, Maria said, "I can't find my magazine. I went to put it away as soon as I got home, but it wasn't in my bag."

"Do you think it fell out?"

Maria shook her head. "I put it in there really carefully and closed the flap before lunch. There's no way it could've fallen out. Besides, I checked as I walked here and there was nothing."

Elisabeth confirmed that she hadn't seen it either while she had managed the whole clean-up after the Haibachs had left.

"Wait—your father picked up your satchel. Does he remember if it was in there?"

"Tata was certain my satchel felt really light." Maria started wringing her hands, and Elisabeth knew she wanted to say something but was scared to.

"What's wrong?" she asked.

Maria stared at the ground. "Is there, I mean, is it possible at all that...maybe one of your siblings took it?"

Anger rose in Elisabeth—how could her best friend accuse a member of her family of stealing? But her anger disappeared as quickly as it had come. She knew her siblings: they would misbehave at the drop of a hat if it suited them. Although she had yet to catch any of them ever lying about something, that didn't mean they never had. She sighed.

"You might be right. I'll try to find out."

CHAPTER THREE

"Will you stop it already?" Jasmine asked, smiling. "You're making me nervous with all your shaking!"

Juliana could only apologize. At her old dance studio in Calgary, if the dancers did well at a competition, Miss Kasia would order in pizza and they'd have a movie night. Jasmine, Juliana's closest—but still new—friend at Kitchener Dance Academy, had explained this studio's traditions: They gave out special, fun awards here! As usual, Juliana couldn't contain her emotions and her legs kept bouncing with excitement.

"Seriously," Mackenzie said. "Did you drink ten energy drinks before you came?" She tucked a strip of purple hair behind her ear.

Juliana shrugged but couldn't still her legs. "Sorry. I can't keep my feelings inside."

It was true, and it was why she loved dance so much: it gave her the freedom to express her emotions. The downside to it, though, was that she could rarely stand still when her feelings threatened to burst through her skin if she didn't move. The drive from Calgary to Kitchener before Christmas had been especially torturous.

"We never did special awards like this back at home," Juliana said.

Miss Denise, the tap and jazz teacher, came into the studio, with Mrs. Laing, the head of the office, behind her. Both were carrying large boxes.

Juliana's team had twenty-five dancers, ranging from fourteen to sixteen years of age. When Juliana had first joined, she'd felt intimidated because she was the weakest dancer on the team. Yet for some reason Miss Denise had accepted her. Juliana worked hard to catch up, but she still had a way to go. She knew she wouldn't get any special award this evening, but just the novelty of the tradition was enough to excite her.

Mrs. Laing set down her box on the floor and left again. Miss Denise set hers down on a chair. She smiled at the dancers.

"We did well this weekend," Miss Denise said. "But as you all know, being a team is about more than just doing well; it's about how we help each other, how much fun we have, and how we try to keep each other's spirits up. There were some strong studios there this weekend, and we didn't win top marks all the time, yet we still came home feeling incredible, and it's because of your attitude toward this team."

A whiff of pizza yanked Juliana out of listening to Miss Denise. Mrs. Laing had returned carrying four flat, square, white pizza boxes.

Once everyone grabbed their serving—Juliana took one slice of Hawaiian and one vegetarian slice—Miss Denise began by holding up a small trophy.

"For the best joke of the weekend...Isaac!"

Remembering the joke, everyone burst out laughing. Juliana was surprised at how funny Isaac could be. She didn't know him well, but he was usually polite, almost shy, sort of quiet, and, well, nice. But that was it, just nice. That he'd cracked a joke like he had seemed to have come out of nowhere.

"For the best mistake...Mackenzie!"

"Seriously?" Mackenzie asked as everyone burst into laughter again. "Just because I backed into a prop doesn't mean I get the prize."

"It's how you backed into the prop," Miss Denise said, a hint of mischief in her eyes. "You threw your magic wand into the air, relevéed onto pointe, caught your wand, pointed it at Jasmine, and then lost your balance. It could have come straight out of an old black-and-white comedy sketch."

Despite her apparent grumpiness, Mackenzie accepted the award. The smallest dancer on the team, her onstage personality more than made up for her size. Her off-stage personality was just as large.

"Most hairspray used in one weekend…"

Everyone shouted, "Ben!"

Ben was Mackenzie's twin. He wore his hair long. Even Juliana was amazed by how much hairspray he had used: he never had to curl or braid or straighten or frizz his hair, yet he had singlehandedly emptied a fresh bottle of hairspray over three days.

"It's a good stain remover!" he protested.

Jasmine leaned over to Juliana. "I think he emptied half of it down the toilet," she whispered. Juliana snickered.

"Now, for this one, I don't have a trophy yet," Miss Denise continued. "It's an award I've never given out before, because I've never had a student do this. The trophy will be ready next week." She lifted out a paper certificate. "Juliana, this one goes to you, for bringing along the most tap shoe screws."

Juliana's cheeks burned but she also laughed. Each tap on a shoe was held in place on the sole by three screws. When Juliana was eleven, one of her ball taps had lost two screws while she was on stage, leaving the tap circling around the last screw as she danced. Rachel, her best friend back home, had removed a screw from one of her shoes so Juliana could finish the competition. Since then, Juliana always brought a palm-sized bag of tap shoe screws to all competitions with her. The chances of it happening again were slim, but Juliana didn't like leaving anything up to chance. She accepted the certificate, tapped a little "shuffle off to Buffalo" in her jazz shoes, and then returned to her spot on the floor next to Jasmine.

Miss Denise finished handing out the awards—everyone got one—and then Mrs. Laing brought in a celebration cake.

"Congratulations again," said Miss Denise. "Enjoy, and then we'll do some stretching and light dancing tonight. I don't want to send you all home with stomach cramps."

Jasmine, Mackenzie, Ben, and Juliana sat in a tight circle while they ate their vanilla cake.

"Man, did you see that one group?" Mackenzie asked. "They're our age and they had to dress up like four-leaf clovers. Kind of like when you were that flower a few years ago, Ben."

Ben's cheeks turned red. "Do you have to bring that up again?"

Mackenzie pinched his cheek. "But you were so cute!"

Ben swatted her hand away. "I'd rather be a flower than a worm."

"It was a contemporary piece," Mackenzie countered. "It was too deep for you to fully comprehend."

Juliana and Jasmine laughed at the twins.

"That's what I hate about having a sister," Ben said. "If she wants to get back at you, all she has to do is tell some kind of embarrassing story."

"So, apparently this photo exists of my mom when she was a kid in some kind of embarrassing fluffy costume," Juliana said, "and I'm trying to find it." She described the photo, and everyone laughed.

"Don't do it, Juliana," Ben said, throwing a look at his sister. "Some photos should remain buried."

Everyone laughed again.

"I have to admit, when my grandfather told me about it at first, I just wanted to find it for myself and then give it to Mom, like a fun-but-embarrassing gift. But then at comp this weekend, Mom ran into an old friend who told her how jealous she'd been of Mom back then because of the role she got at their year-end show with that costume. Mom told me she actually wished she still had the picture. My aunt and uncle are pretty sure it's disappeared, but I think it's in the house somewhere. My grandfather at least seems to think so."

"And you've looked?" Jasmine asked.

Juliana nodded. "In the obvious places, but I couldn't find it."

"Then you need an accomplice, someone who knows the family and the house really well, falls under the radar and won't tell your mom."

"Of course you'd suggest that," Juliana said. "Your dad's a cop."

"And cops know how to find things secretly," Jasmine said. "There must be someone."

Juliana knew just the person.

"You're asking someone who's going blind to help you look for something?" Sophie asked.

Juliana was helping Sophie with her math.

"I can do the looking, but you know everyone so much better than I do, and I don't think you're as innocent as you look. I bet you snuck around Opa's house a lot when you were younger. I need a sidekick."

Sophie laughed. "You know how dorky you sound, right?"

Juliana playfully swatted her cousin on the shoulder. "I'm serious! I really need to find this photo. You should've seen the look on Mom's face, Sophie. She actually looked like this photo would make her really happy."

"Uncle Peter did say on Monday he thought Aunt Katy was regretting something."

"Exactly. Mom's been so serious since we've moved here. It'd be fun to find this and hear her laugh."

Aunt Anne opened the door to Sophie's room. "I'm hearing a little too much fun and not enough studying."

The girls apologized and then Juliana asked, "Can Sophie come over tomorrow after school? I want to find that photo of Mom."

Aunt Anne gave Juliana a quizzical look.

"She knows Opa's house better than me," Juliana said.

Aunt Anne placed her hands on her hips. "Well, so do I," she said playfully.

"Any ideas?" Juliana asked.

"Wall unit in the—"

"—living room," Juliana finished for her. "Already checked there, and in the kitchen, my closet, the closet in the guest bedroom, and my parents' closet."

"Your parents' closet?"

Juliana shrugged. "Yeah, why? There's nothing in there I can't see."

"Okay..." Aunt Anne thought for a few more minutes and then shook her head. "I still think Katy threw it out. But if it makes you feel like Nancy Drew, then go for it. But get your homework done first."

Juliana didn't know who Nancy Drew was, but Sophie seemed to. Juliana would ask her later.

"But if that ice storm hits tomorrow," Aunt Anne said, one foot out the door, "then you may have to postpone your sleuthing."

"We'll be fine," Juliana said. "They said there was only a ten percent chance that we'd get it."

THE NEXT MORNING, AT TEN, AUNT ANNE BROUGHT SOPHIE over.

"Cool sunglasses," Juliana said to Sophie, but Sophie didn't look pleased. She stepped inside, left her boots on the tiny landing, walked up to the kitchen, and set the sunglasses on the small countertop under the side window.

Behind Sophie's back, Aunt Anne rolled her eyes and shook her head. "You two," she said, still standing outside the door at the side of the house. "I almost broke a hip walking over here."

"I salted!" Juliana said.

The ice storm had indeed hit early morning, cancelling all school buses and closing all schools. Juliana would normally take a day like today to study and get ahead in her schoolwork, but the idea of searching for the photo was too enticing. Besides, with Dad on the road again, Mom at the grocery store, and Opa still in Cuba, Juliana could snoop around.

Aunt Anne smiled. "You only did your portion of the sidewalk. I'll be back at lunch." Aunt Anne shuffled back down the driveway. "It's days like today where I wish I'd done figure skating instead of dance!" she shouted back. "And Sophie—wear your sunglasses if you go outside!"

"Whatever," Sophie said, though not loud enough for her mom to hear.

Juliana closed the door behind her aunt.

"Everything okay?" Juliana asked as Sophie slid out of her coat.

"I just hate wearing sunglasses."

"Oh...okay." Juliana had never met anyone before who hated wearing sunglasses. Worried it had something to do with Sophie's eyes, though, Juliana let the topic drop. "Something to drink?" she asked.

"Nope." Sophie took off her hat and mitts and went to hang everything in the hallway closet around the corner from the kitchen. When she returned, she was again the bright, happy girl Juliana knew. "Let's get started. You said yesterday where you've already checked. Where do we start then?"

Juliana's expression turned grim. "I think we need to start with the cellar," she said.

"You mean the dungeon," Sophie replied. "We always called it the dungeon when I was little."

Changing its name from cellar to dungeon sent shivers up Juliana's spine. She had only been down there once, at Christmas, soon after she and her family had arrived. It was the only place she could escape to when everyone was wanting her to be this polite, perfect, little daughter even though she had just been ripped away from her life back home.

"Okay," she said, taking a deep breath. "But it's gross in there."

"You're looking," Sophie said, a huge smile on her face, "I'm the sidekick."

"That is so not fair," Juliana said, a mock-sarcastic tone in her voice.

"Your words, not mine," Sophie replied and gestured to Juliana to go first.

The stairs to the basement creaked, something they always did, but this time their sounds made Juliana shudder. So far as she knew, Opa had never cleaned the rec room and cellar since Oma died. Juliana had helped Mom clean the rec room after they arrived so Juliana could have a place to practise, but they had never tackled the cellar.

At the bottom of the stairs, the door to the rec room and therefore the gateway to the dungeon stood ominously before them, as though it were hiding some dangerous treasure.

"Rebecca used to tell me that Bloody Mary lived in there," Sophie said.

"That's a horrible thing to tell a young sister!"

"I know. But that's Rebecca for you."

Juliana opened the door. The cream shag carpet, peeling wallpaper, and 1970s furniture—orange, brown, and puke green—had seen better days. However, Juliana had come to love the worn, retro feel to the room.

"How many times did Rebecca tell you that you had say 'Bloody Mary' before she'd appear in the mirror and trap you in it?" Juliana asked.

Sophie shivered. "Three."

"Wow, that's short. I'd heard thirteen."

The door to the dungeon was to their left. Next to it was a bar covered in orange vinyl with large, black, vinyl buttons. Juliana had a hard time imagining why anyone had ever thought that would look good.

"Wait a minute," Juliana said. "I don't recall seeing a mirror when I was in there at Christmas—"

Sophie laughed. "Maybe it's not there anymore. But maybe there are more dead spiders? Remember when Dean took one out of your hair?"

"Don't remind me!" Juliana shook the icky feeling out through her hands. "That was so gross!"

The girls' feet wouldn't move past the rec room doorway.

"Your sidekick suggests we start with a cleaner room," Sophie said finally. "How about the laundry room?"

"Perfect."

Juliana closed the door to the rec room and flicked on the light in the laundry room to their right. The room had brown wood panelling all around it, and a tiny window sat high up on the left. Juliana felt a twinge of sadness at the washing machine and dryer ahead of them. One time she had seen Opa, overtaken by his dementia, carrying a stack of clean tea towels from the kitchen to the laundry room to wash. A loud bang on one of the machines, followed by the German word Uncle Peter had used the other day had brought Juliana downstairs where she had discovered that the washer's child lock had been turned on. Opa had obviously done this before.

"I think there's a closet in here somewhere," Sophie said, "but it's small. To our left, under the stairs?"

Juliana looked and confirmed Sophie's memory: hidden behind some old boxes was indeed a small closet that had been built under the stairs, its doors covered in more wood panelling. Juliana pushed the boxes out of the way. The closet was a little shorter than her. She opened its doors slowly—she didn't want to be startled by anything dead—and looked in.

"Well?" Sophie asked.

"Do you see a flashlight anywhere? It's dark in here."

"Um, Juliana..."

Juliana turned around. "Sorry—I still don't know what you—"

"I get it. It's okay." A hint of sadness flickered across her face.

Juliana felt sorry for Sophie. She didn't know what she would do if she lost her eyesight. How would she dance if she couldn't see? Juliana stuck her head into the closet, trying to angle her body to avoid blocking the light.

"There are tons of boxes down there, I think all the way to the bottom of the stairs. Some seem to have scraps of fabric in them. Some are really small. I don't know, maybe puzzles or games." Juliana sneezed. "Yuck. Too much dust.

But I can't get in there. Either you get in there to get them out—because you're smaller—or we leave it."

"Leave it."

Juliana agreed, sneezed again, closed the closet, pushed the larger boxes back into place, and joined Sophie by the door.

"The dungeon's our last spot in the house then," Juliana said.

Both girls looked at each other.

"Well, I've been in there once before," Juliana said. "It can't be worse the second time, right?"

"Right," Sophie said.

Juliana turned off the light in the laundry room and the girls opened the door into the rec room.

"Okay," Juliana said. "Now...one of us has to open that door." She paused. "Why don't you open it and I'll look."

"Um, yeah, no. Remember? I don't have to search, and opening the door is related to searching."

Juliana took a deep breath and gathered her courage. "Fine. Then I'll open the door."

"You can do it!" Sophie suddenly cheered. "I believe in you, Juliana!"

Juliana turned back around and raised an eyebrow. "Really?"

Sophie grinned and shrugged. "I'm not searching, but I can be your personal cheerleader!"

Juliana shook her head in playful disbelief. "Sheesh,"

she said. She gripped the door handle, turned it, closed her eyes, and pulled the door open.

"And?" Sophie asked.

"My eyes are closed."

"Seriously? That's my problem! Open them!"

Juliana lifted her eyelids a crack. Seeing no decaying bugs on the floor immediately ahead of her, she stepped inside.

"Oh god, it's so gross in here," she said. The cold cement floor sent shivers up her body and she hesitated to pull the string on the light bulb. But she knew she had to. "Okay, I'm turning on the light now," she reported.

She pulled the string, the light turned on, she saw a spider, shrieked...and then the power to the basement went out.

CHAPTER FOUR

lisabeth finished brushing out Rosina's hair and then braided it as the siblings prepared for the night. Luki was already in bed, and Anna was trying to brush her own hair, wincing at every pull.

Elisabeth had searched all three rooms in the house and had found nothing. She hoped her siblings wouldn't have stolen Maria's prized possession. Had they not learned anything from Pastor Fröhlich's teachings in church? The seventh commandment forbade stealing. *Thou shalt not steal.* God's Word was clear.

"Maria came by again later this afternoon," Elisabeth said. "She couldn't find her magazine. Did anyone take it?"

Rosina whipped her head around so fast that Elisabeth had to let go of her braid.

"I don't steal," she said.

Elisabeth was taken aback by Rosina's sharp reaction. "I suppose that means you didn't take it." How was Elisabeth supposed to figure out if someone was telling a lie? "What about you, Anna? You like to bother me."

Anna crossed her arms, tilted her chin down and looked at Elisabeth from under her eyelashes.

She's not saying she didn't, Elisabeth thought. *But she often gives me looks like that.*

She sighed. "Luki?"

Her brother frantically shook his head from side to side.

Would Mammi take it? Mammi had asked the girls to close the magazine and had said it had been a waste of time. A few moments later, the children had disobeyed Mammi—and therefore had also disobeyed God's fourth commandment, to honour one's parents. *No*, Elisabeth thought. *She would never steal, especially after Maria put it away herself. Besides, she never left the table during lunch. But each of my siblings did.*

After the children were tucked in and Elisabeth had read a story from the Bible, she lay down on the straw-filled mattress of her bed. Mammi would join them soon—she was washing herself in the kitchen. Could Elisabeth ask Mammi for help with this? *No, Mammi already has too much to worry about*, she thought. She glanced up at the crucifix that hung above the door. *Can You tell me who's lying?* she asked.

As usual, Jesus silently stared down at her, not giving her an answer.

IT WAS EARLY MONDAY MORNING—THE SUN WAS JUST beginning to rise—and already the Schuhmacher household was in motion. Luki entered from the house door, dusting himself off after having fed the cows and horses. Anna followed, also cleaning herself up quickly. She had fed the chickens, ducks, geese, and pigs. They took off their full aprons, and Anna tied on a fresh one that started at the waist and complemented her dress. Elisabeth handed them their school bags and sent them off.

"Rosina," she called into the front room. "Georg and Stefan will be here shortly. Are you ready?"

"I'm not going," her sister replied.

Elisabeth sighed and decided not to argue. Rosina would be going, whether she liked it or not, because Mammi needed to repair shoes in Tata's workshop out back and therefore couldn't keep an eye on her youngest child. Rosina had to come with Elisabeth while she worked on the family's fields with help from Georg and Stefan.

A half-hour later, Elisabeth heard a horse and wagon pull up in front of their house. She peeked out the window: Georg sat on the horse and Stefan sat in the wagon.

Georg was a big man. He was a blacksmith just like his

father, Tata's brother, whom Elisabeth called Konrad-Bátschi. At roughly twice Elisabeth's age, Georg had fought in the war, and instead of coming home a hero, had survived the war a "broken" man, as Stefan had once described his friend. Once one of the most feared men in the village, Georg had become a shadow of his former self: he was quiet, withdrawn, and a slave to his mind which repeated nightmares so frightening and so real to Georg that he reacted to them as though they were really happening.

Stefan was almost the opposite of Georg: sociable and funny. However, during his time in the war he had lost most of one arm—how, Elisabeth didn't know—and had been captured by the Russians. He had only returned the month before, after spending two years in a prisoner-of-war camp in Siberia. The deprivations and physical labour had left him looking like a gangly boy whose body had grown faster than his appetite could keep up.

"Rosina, time to go to the *salasch*. We don't want to keep them waiting."

A *salasch* was a large piece of farmland with a house on it—much like the house most Germans had in the village —that was occupied by the caretakers of the fields. When Tata's and Konrad-Bátschi's father was still alive, he had given most of his *salasch* to Konrad-Bátschi, the eldest of his two sons, leaving Tata and his family with just enough land to feed themselves. Elisabeth had never understood how a father could treat his sons so unfairly especially when the custom was to divide the land equally between all sons.

"I'm not going," Rosina insisted.

"Fine. Then wait while I ask Mammi if you can stay," Elisabeth said, betting her sister would insist on doing it herself. Rosina often did the opposite of what she was told, and Elisabeth hoped she would do that now.

"*I'm* asking her," Rosina said and stomped out of the house.

Pleased with herself, Elisabeth tapped on a window in the front room and waved to the men. Stefan waved back and Georg nodded his greeting. She grabbed her bag, which contained extra blankets and shawls, and walked out in time to see Rosina trudging back toward her.

Did she ever stop stomping? Elisabeth wondered and immediately asked Jesus for forgiveness for her angry thoughts.

"It's not fair!" Rosina shouted.

"Rosina!" Elisabeth said through clenched teeth. "They can hear you."

"I want my doll. Then we may go."

Elisabeth rolled her eyes as Rosina continued stamping her feet as she entered the house, but Rosina found the doll she had received for Christmas and then followed Elisabeth, still grumbling as she went.

"Good day!" Stefan said, removing his hat as they

reached the wagon. His smile immediately brightened Elisabeth's mood.

"Good day," she replied, smiling back.

Rosina at first said nothing. Instead she stood still, staring at Stefan's missing arm. Elisabeth nudged her and out flew a "Hello" as quiet as a butterfly, though Rosina's eyes didn't move.

Stefan jumped out of the wagon and helped both girls in as best he could. He was finally putting on a little weight, but it would take many meals before he looked like a grown man again.

Georg turned around to see that everyone had found a seat, his face still as usual. Rosina scrambled as far away from him as she could, pushing her spine into a corner of the wagon and pulling up her knees. Elisabeth's face turned red. Georg snapped the reins and the wagon lurched into motion, the gravel crackling under the wagon's wheels and the horse's hooves clip-clopping in a steady rhythm.

"What did you do after church yesterday?" Stefan asked.

Elisabeth told him about Sunday: Maria's family's visit, the magazine, and the shoes. She stole a glance at Rosina and then whispered to Stefan, "I think one of my siblings took it and is lying about it."

"What did you say?" Rosina asked. "I can't hear you."

"Nothing for your ears," Elisabeth said.

Rosina's eyes narrowed as her gaze traveled between Stefan and Elisabeth. "You said something about the magazine. I know you did. I didn't steal it." She stamped her foot on the wagon floor, prompting Georg to turn around from his perch on the horse.

Rosina pulled her knees in tighter. "Maybe Georg stole it!"

Georg turned back around.

But to Elisabeth's surprise, Stefan laughed.

"Isn't it funny, Georg?" he shouted up to his friend. "The thought of you taking a women's magazine?"

Georg didn't turn around but shrugged slightly.

Elisabeth tried to keep a serious face to show Rosina she disapproved of her behaviour, but the more she tried to tighten her lips, the harder it was not to smile: the thought of big, strong Georg perusing a women's magazine broke through her resolve and she laughed with Stefan. Even Rosina giggled.

Elisabeth exchanged kisses with Deaf Lissi, wife to Georg's brother, Samuel. She wasn't actually deaf—the nickname had been passed down through the family from an ancestor who had been hard of hearing. But with so many Elisabeths in the congregation and especially in the Schuhmacher family—it was also Mammi's first name—nicknames helped keep everyone straight. Samuel and Deaf Lissi lived in the homestead on the family *salasch*.

The homestead on the *salasch* was similar to houses in the village: white walls and blue gables on the outside and two rooms on the inside with a kitchen in between. However, the back room, instead of being formally decorated to receive visitors, was sparsely furnished and used for tasks like weaving or making brooms. Behind the homestead were the stalls for the cows and horses followed by the smaller ones for the pigs. Konrad-Bátschi's family raised animals for themselves and to sell at the market on Tuesdays, something Elisabeth's family couldn't do with the size of their portion of the land.

However, no German rightfully owned a home and did not adorn it with flowers. A fenced-in garden already beginning to blossom with tiny snowdrops lay in front of Samuel's home.

Samuel limped as he pulled two horses attached to a plough out of the stalls of the *salasch*. Elisabeth knew he had had polio in childhood.

"I'm sorry I don't get to see you often, anymore," he called to Elisabeth as he got closer, doffing his cap. "But the *salasch* needs me and my wife now."

Elisabeth nodded in return. "I understand," she said, a smile on her face. "The distance from here to the village is too much to travel every day." Indeed, she already found that the four kilometres to the fields and back took up too much of her day: over two hours.

The animals snorted and neighed, and Rosina rushed behind Elisabeth, who placed her arm around her young sister: horses used to scare Elisabeth, too. As a child, she had even woken up occasionally from a nightmare in which a horse had fallen on her. It had never happened to her in real life but the tall animals, with their barrel-like bodies and long faces, simply scared her then. But she had eventually learned to love them.

"Rosina can help me in the house," Deaf Lissi offered and held out her hand for her young cousin. Rosina didn't hesitate to accept.

"We'll begin ploughing your fields today," Georg said.

Samuel handed Elisabeth the horses' reins so he and his brother could inspect the plough and tethers.

The more time Elisabeth spent with Georg, the harder she found it to understand Mammi's refusal to let him help them. Mammi had even grumbled when Georg, Samuel, and Stefan had shown up last week to transfer her family's dung pile into a wagon to carry out to their fields. But who else was going to do it?

"Thank you," Elisabeth said. "You've really been a blessing to our family."

Georg paused for a moment and looked at Elisabeth, but she couldn't tell what the expression on his face meant. Was he about to smile? His lips tightened slightly as though they wanted to curve upwards. Samuel patted his brother on the back, which brought an annoyed look to Georg's face. Elisabeth smiled: Samuel had done it once before in front of her and had said that Georg hated it. A moment later, though, Georg's face returned to its usual stillness that left Elisabeth wondering how much of him was here on earth and how much in heaven.

"I'll bring out the second plough shortly and then Stefan can help guide the animals," Samuel said. "My brother inspected it yesterday, so it's ready to go."

As her cousins continued their inspection, Elisabeth stroked the horse's mane, trying to figure out which of her siblings had stolen Maria's precious magazine. She remembered that Rosina had chosen to knit in the front room, Luki had stepped outside to look after the animals, and Anna had needed the outhouse. All three had gone through the kitchen where Maria's satchel had lain. Any one of them could've taken the magazine. *Anna and Rosina had fallen in love with the modern designs. It can't have been Luki*, she thought. *He likes Mammi's shoes.*

"Elisabeth?"

She jumped and one horse pulled its head back in response. Stefan had called her. "Yes?" She blushed. "Sorry."

"Are you still thinking about who took that magazine?"

Elisabeth nodded. "I don't see why Luki would take it," she began, continuing her thoughts as though Stefan had heard the first ones. "He says he doesn't think Mammi should make special shoes. But Rosina wanted to knit squares for them—" Stefan made a quizzical face at the suggestion—"and Anna wants to embroider the shoes, so she would love to study the magazine for designs, but she's also angry at me for telling her she has to help more. She's nice to visitors, but to me she's horrid—she'd steal the magazine just to embarrass me in front of my friend."

Stefan shrugged and smiled. "I don't know your brother and sisters well, so I'm afraid I'm not much help. But I'm sure you'll find it."

Georg crouched down beside the plough and scraped dried dirt off one of its two shares. "Why is this magazine so important?"

His attention to such a topic surprised her. Georg usually spoke only when necessary.

"Aside from the fact that it's not mine," she said, "it has pictures of modern shoes in it. I'm certain Mammi could make them, but she wants to uphold tradition." She described the shoes from the magazine. "And there were also these—I don't know what you would call them—they go over shoes and have buttons up the side. They go perhaps a few inches above the ankle. They look so..."

"Modern?" Samuel offered as he tugged down on a buckle.

Elisabeth nodded. "Yes."

The horses moved and Georg pulled his hands back so they would not be sliced by the plough. Elisabeth stroked the horses' muzzles and spoke to them to calm them down. Once the animals and tool were still again, Georg continued his work. "I would buy shoes like that for Eva," he said. "She deserves something nice. I know she would wear them to the dances." Eva was Georg's wife. She and Elisabeth had developed a new bond as Elisabeth tried to understand what was torturing Georg. At only eighteen years of age, she was much closer to Elisabeth's fourteen years than she was to her husband's twenty-nine years. However, that was normal for a second wife. Georg's first wife and child had died from a fever while he was away at war.

"Rosina can help with picking up the remaining stubble in your fields from last year," Elisabeth said, changing the subject to the cut-off remains of last year's cornstalks. She took two steps toward the homestead and stopped. Rosina would simply disobey her again if she called for her. She turned to face her cousin. "Georg, I need your help," she said. "Can you get my sister for me? She won't listen to me if I ask her to come out."

Georg nodded and headed into the house.

"He seems much calmer," Elisabeth said to Stefan and Samuel.

"There's no one to stare at him out here," Stefan said.

"Lissa doesn't like him," Samuel said of his wife, "but

she tolerates him. He's often all right out here, so long as Tata..."

He left his sentence unfinished, but everyone knew what he was going to say: So long as Konrad-Bátschi stayed in the village. Elisabeth had witnessed on several occasions her uncle belittle and beat his son. He had once even said in front of a crowd that he wished Georg hadn't returned from the war.

"But it's also the ride," Stefan added.

Samuel nodded. "He learned how to ride a horse while at war. Once his saddle came in from Arad, he's always insisted on riding the horse instead of sitting in the wagon and driving."

Elisabeth had noticed that, too. Rarely did anyone else in the village actually sit on a horse; they drove from the wagon.

"He jumps at every chance he can get to ride," Stefan said.

Samuel broke out into a grin. "My brother jumping?"

Stefan slapped Samuel playfully on the shoulder. "You know what I mean. He takes any opportunity to ride a horse out here. He'd probably even bring me a clean fork so Deaf Lissi didn't have to wash dishes."

Rosina ran out of the house, interrupting the men's gentle teasing. "Help!" she cried. "He's chasing me!"

The exaggerated fear on her face, coupled with the jokes the men had just exchanged, meant the laughter continued. Even Georg wore a quiet smile on his face as he strolled out of the house behind her. Rosina clamped her arms around Elisabeth's waist, almost pulling both of them to the ground, which only added to the men's amusement. Rosina scowled.

"They aren't laughing at you," Elisabeth said to her sister.

"We're not," Samuel said. "We're sorry, Rosi. We were laughing at Georg."

Georg raised an eyebrow. "But I was in the house."

Samuel flashed his brother a big smile. "We know."

Elisabeth clapped her hands together. "All right, you men, time to get to work." She looked down at Rosina, whose arms were still wrapped around her. "You, too." As she pulled Rosina's hands away from her, Elisabeth saw a spider crawling up her shoe. "But not you," she said to it and crouched down. "You don't belong here." She coaxed it onto her hand, cupped her hands together, and while the spider tickled her palms, carried it over to a tree where it could be safe and released it.

"It's a spider," Stefan said. "You just kill it."

"Or let it live its life as it was meant to," Elisabeth replied. She brushed her hands on her apron. "Safe and sound."

CHAPTER FIVE

"Oh my god oh my god oh my god! Where's that spider?! I can't tell what I'm stepping on!" Juliana shrieked as she tried to turn around. The rec room was almost pitch black because snow and ice blocked any light from coming through the tiny windows.

"If it crunches, it's a bug," Sophie said.

"That so does not help! Come closer and reach out your hand."

"Ew! And step on bugs?"

"Of course not! Stay on the carpet, reach out your hand, and then I'll try and find it."

If Juliana were upstairs, she would've heard her cousin taking two steps toward her; the floors creaked that much. But on shag carpet, Juliana could hear nothing.

"Are you there?" Juliana swung her hand back and forth.

"Yes," Sophie said. "Listen," and she snapped her fingers.

Locating the sound, Juliana grabbed Sophie's hand and took a small leap out the door. "I've never been so thankful for carpet in my life," she said.

The girls felt their way along the wall and out the rec room door. They knew the stairs were straight ahead, and a little daylight shone down to the landing from the kitchen windows.

The side door opened and both girls shrieked again.

It was Mom.

She laughed at her daughter and niece. "What's going on?" she asked. "You're all jittery."

Juliana thought fast. "The lights went out while we were downstairs."

Mom placed her hands on her hips. "That much I can gather. But you're usually cool as a cucumber during blackouts."

"There was a spider," Juliana said. Mom nodded. Juliana breathed a sigh of relief. She had avoided lying.

"I put our flashlights on a shelf in the laundry room," Mom said.

"Now you tell me!"

Sophie spoke up. "Juliana was going to show me some of her dances from the competition I couldn't go to."

"You were going to show her full dances on your tiny tap board?" Mom raised an eyebrow.

"Um, why are you home?" Juliana asked, hoping the change in subject would distract Mom and give the girls a chance to escape to Juliana's room.

"The grocery store closed an hour ago, because we couldn't get enough staff in. You'd think this was Florida with snow the way Ontarians act when there's a little ice. But with hardly any staff and no customers coming, we shut down, and it's a good thing, too, now that the power's out."

"Nice to have you home, Aunt Katy," Sophie said.

The two girls darted off for Juliana's room before Mom had a chance to say anything else.

Juliana closed the door behind them and invited Sophie to sit down on her bed with her.

"Show you my dances?" she asked Sophie. "In that tiny space?"

Sophie shrugged.

Juliana ran her fingers through her hair. "Okay, so what do we know so far about the photo?"

"We know we can't find it," Sophie said.

Juliana rolled her eyes. "I know that, Einstein. But there are a few things we do know."

"No one knows where it is."

"And your mom and Uncle Peter think my mom tossed it."

"But your mom would've told you that, right?"

"Yeah. I mean, if she was that angry about it, you'd think she'd remember tearing it up or something."

The girls sat in silence for a few minutes, thinking.

"I've checked pretty much everywhere already," Juliana said. "And we checked the laundry room."

"That leaves the dungeon and garage."

"And Opa's room."

"We can't look through all his belongings," Sophie said. "We'd get in trouble for that."

Juliana nodded. "True..."

Or was it? Juliana just needed an excuse to go down there. Then all she had to do was not get caught.

JULIANA REACHED UP FOR THE CEILING TO STRETCH. AFTER Sophie had left and Juliana had had lunch, she had attempted to do some homework with the bit of daylight that had shone through her window. But she had fallen asleep, only to wake up now. The clock in her room flashed 12:00 but the one on her phone displayed 3:36.

"Awake?" Mom asked as she came out of hers and Dad's bedroom carrying a basket of laundry. "Good. You can take this to Opa's room."

"Sure!" *That was easy*, she thought.

Mom stopped dead in her tracks. "Something's definitely wrong with you," she said.

Uh oh. Too happy, Juliana realized. She tilted her head to one side. "Really, Mom. Don't you think I can, you know, not complain about chores for a change? I mean, did you ever think that maybe we had such an awesome time together at the competition that I might want to help out a little more?" She lifted the laundry basket out of Mom's hands, trying hard to avoid the suspicious look coming from Mom's eyes. Juliana feigned a pout and swung her hair as she turned on her heel. "I can be helpful!"

Mom chuckled as Juliana walked down the hallway and into the kitchen. *That was definitely too much*, Juliana thought. Then her body filled with dread. *What if she makes me wash lettuce next?* Washing lettuce was Juliana's most hated household chore. She vowed to act more normal later. Hopefully that would get rid of Mom's suspicion. *First Aunt Anne needs me to lie to Mom about the party, and now I have to lie about the photo.* Juliana didn't want to be the one to ruin either surprise but it was hard to lie about something she could hardly wait to tell Mom about.

She carried the laundry down the stairs, feeling a pang of guilt as she entered Opa's messy room. Well, it wasn't messy to him; he had told her once that he found it easier to find things if they were all spread out. It would make it harder for her to search here, but given his faulty memory, it made no sense to wait until he got home. He likely still didn't remember where the photo was anyway.

Juliana searched through Opa's room as she put his laundry away, checking the wardrobe, the drawer at the bottom of the wardrobe, the drawers under his bed, and his closet. There was still a chest she had to go through. At least putting his laundry away gave her the excuse she needed to look through things: she didn't know where stuff belonged.

She opened the bottom drawer of the dresser.

"What's this?" she asked out loud as she lifted up a long braid of hair. "What's Opa doing with a hairpiece?" Half intrigued and half disgusted, she put it back. It was a mystery that would have to wait for another day. She closed the drawer and opened the next one just as she heard the latch in the door open. Juliana banged the drawer shut and whipped around.

"Mom," she said. "I'm just—"

But the look on Mom's face told Juliana that she didn't care what her daughter was about to say. Mom's eyes opened wide as she scanned Opa's small bedroom, inch by inch.

"My lord..."

Was it really a big deal? Rachel's room was a mess like

this all the time. "I know you don't like things messy, Mom, but he says it helps him find things."

Mom didn't respond. She lifted up a sweater, smelled its armpits—Juliana wrinkled her nose—and lay it over her arm. Mom inspected more clothing, piece by piece, folding some and putting it away and collecting others over her arm. Juliana stepped out of Mom's way and watched. Was she supposed to help? She didn't want to smell armpits: that was worse than walking into the dungeon. In fact, she'd rather wash lettuce.

Juliana had never seen Mom like this before. Her face shifted between anger, sadness, confusion, and fear. Whenever Mom was angry at Juliana, Juliana knew: Mom yelled. She rarely saw Mom sad, and never scared. *And she's only confused when she talks to me*, she thought jokingly. But this was no joke. Mom was clearly concerned about Opa but Juliana still didn't understand why.

The pile over Mom's arm looked like it was about to tip. Juliana placed the last few clean items on Opa's bed and held the empty laundry basket out to Mom. Mom dumped the clothing in without a word and continued picking things up and putting away whatever seemed clean. Juliana stood in the middle of the room, the heavy basket in her arms, and offered it whenever Mom handed clothing to her.

After five minutes of watching, Juliana had to break the silence. "What's wrong?"

Mom stopped. "I'm..." She stared at the basket Juliana

held. The floor of Opa's bedroom was now clean, revealing the same cream shag carpet from the rec room. "I'm sorry. I...I heard you but I didn't. What did he say?" Juliana repeated what Opa had told her about why he kept his clothing everywhere. Mom took the basket out of Juliana's hands, sadness remaining on her face. "When did he tell you this?"

Juliana needed a moment to think back. "I don't know. Maybe last month? Mom? Is everything okay?"

After another minute of silence, Mom's emotions changed again. She furrowed her eyebrows and straightened her shoulders, like a dancer summoning her confidence before stepping onstage.

"This is why he didn't want me doing his laundry. He knows this is one of the symptoms that show things have been getting worse. He's been hiding it from me." Mom turned on her heel and marched out the door. She slid the laundry basket across the laundry room floor so hard it banged against the dryer. "I have to call Anne and Peter," she said, her voice disappearing as she strode up the stairs.

A twinge of guilt tugged at Juliana's stomach. But it wasn't because she had been caught snooping—she wasn't sure if Mom had even registered that. The guilt came from her not having told Mom earlier about Opa's room.

"I really did think his excuse made sense," she said to no one.

Sitting at her desk, her laptop open, Juliana clicked on the bookmark for a website about dementia and scrolled through to the list of symptoms of the early stages of the disease. She had read this list once before but had avoided it ever since. It had told her Opa's future, and she didn't want to see it.

The look on Mom's face had told Juliana that maybe she needed to know more. What if Opa again did something that looked normal but really wasn't?

She read the symptoms of early-stage dementia, and sure enough, there it was: "People living with dementia may leave their clothing on chairs and floors so they can find them more easily."

Juliana stared at that last part of the sentence and repeated it over in her mind, an idea formulating as she did so: *...so they can find them more easily.* What if Mom and Dad changed Opa's closet to help him find things more easily? Juliana promised herself that she would talk to Mom about it later.

CHAPTER SIX

"Thank you," Elisabeth said to Georg and Stefan as she stood on the road in front of her house again. Rosina had awoken as soon as the wagon had reached the Schuhmacher home, and no sooner had Stefan helped her over the wagon's side than she ran into the home, looking back to see if Georg was following. "And please thank Deaf Lissi again for feeding us," Elisabeth added. "Her cooking is wonderful."

Georg nodded and Stefan smiled. Stefan climbed back into the wagon, Georg snapped the reins, and the horse and wagon pulled away. Elisabeth walked through the front gate and took one look back.

Stefan did, too.

Elisabeth blushed as she entered the front yard, then the poultry yard, and then turned to her left to reach her home's entrance. But whatever unfamiliar feelings Stefan awakened in her disappeared at the welcome sight of a chair in the kitchen. She collapsed into it, her bag dropping beside her on the floor. She had forgotten how tiring a day on the fields was. *I've become too lazy this winter*, she thought.

"I'm hungry!" Rosina complained.

Elisabeth sighed. How was she going to handle all of this? As much as she enjoyed spending time with the men —she preferred their talk of politics and world events to women's and girls' gossip—she didn't know how she was going to take care of her family's land, the household, and her siblings at the same time. Because Tata was faster at making shoes than Mammi was, he could take time off to help with the fields when it was needed. Rosina had helped with planting seeds as soon as her tiny fingers could hold them, but she still moved at a snail's pace compared to Elisabeth.

It was already late afternoon, and Elisabeth still had to prepare supper. She also needed to begin preparing the kitchen garden, which itself was large. Turning the dung into the soil alone took at least half a day and that was with adult help.

"I had some bread," Anna replied from the front room, surprising Elisabeth. Elisabeth craned her neck to the right and saw Anna playing with dried cobs of corn and her doll. Of course she was home—school was over for the day.

That meant Luki was probably in the workshop with Mammi.

"Couldn't you at least be outside preparing the garden or peeling potatoes in here?" Elisabeth asked. Why did everyone wait for her to tell them what to do?

"My ankle hurts," Anna said. "A boy kicked it on my way home."

Elisabeth mustered whatever energy she had to stand up. She was not going to let Anna get away with this. "You realize God will punish you if you're lying."

"I'm not lying!"

"Which ankle is it?"

"My right one."

Elisabeth dragged herself into the front room to look at it. Rosina retrieved her doll and dried cobs of corn from their small basket of toys and immediately joined Anna.

Anna looks too excited and happy to have a sore ankle, Elisabeth thought. Then she got an idea. "I guess you'll have to rest in bed. If your ankle hurts, you need to put it up. That means you won't be able to play with the Bartolfs later this afternoon after your chores."

Anna scowled. "I'm fine if I sit at the table. It doesn't hurt here."

Elisabeth continued to play along. "All right, then." She walked to the corner of the room where the sewing basket was kept along with clothing that needed to be mended. "Then you can sew up the holes in these clothes." She dropped the basket on the table and smiled at Anna whose scowl grew even deeper.

Elisabeth's confidence swelled: she was finally understanding how to handle her siblings without threatening them with physical punishment. Now she just needed to get Rosina onto her side.

"Since your ankle hurts," she continued, "I guess that means Rosina will have to help me in the garden."

"But I want to help Mammi make the shoes pretty!" Rosina said.

Elisabeth shook her head. "I'm sorry, Rosina, but not only do we not have the magazine with the beautiful pictures in it, the garden must be prepared. Anna says she can't, so that leaves you. Unless her ankle doesn't really hurt..." But no sooner had the words slid out of Elisabeth's mouth than she knew she'd pushed too far.

"No!" Rosina stomped her foot on the ground and marched past Elisabeth, through the kitchen, and out the door toward the workshop.

Elisabeth sighed and Anna smiled. Elisabeth's plan to force Anna to admit her ankle felt fine had failed, and now Rosina was angry with Elisabeth.

What about you? she asked Jesus. *Did You have any siblings?*

~

AN HOUR LATER, AFTER MAMMI HAD STEPPED IN TO HELP SET things straight and force both of the younger sisters to help inside, Elisabeth had to turn the beds in the kitchen garden by herself. She shovelled dung from her wheelbarrow onto the bed, used a rake to spread it out, then drove the tip of the spade into the soil, and turned it over, one spadeful after the next.

"Elisabeth?"

She looked up and saw Stefan at the gate to the property.

"May I come in?"

She nodded. Her heart beat as though she was scared, but she wasn't. She no longer felt compelled to stare at his missing arm, so she wasn't scared of embarrassing herself. Why was she feeling this way?

"I thought I'd come to see if I can help with anything else," he said. "I would've said something earlier, but I wanted to see if my parents needed me first. They're working on the Haibach farm with a few others this year, though, so they have more help."

Elisabeth wiped her brow. "How can you have this much energy? I'm ready to fall asleep."

"We didn't have a choice in the camp," he replied.

Now Elisabeth's cheeks did burn with embarrassment. "I'm sorry. I didn't mean to ask about—"

Stefan waved her apology away. "There's nothing you could have done about it. I'm glad just to have a real bed and unending days of enough food. But I promised you several weeks ago that I would help. I don't want to be paid, I just want a chance to prove myself. Do you have another spade?"

Elisabeth again tried to protest. The kitchen garden was women's work. What would Mammi say if she saw her accepting help from a man, let alone one who wasn't a relative? But Elisabeth glanced over the garden: she had many square metres to turn, and it would take her several days at this rate, given everything else she had to tend. Stefan continued to insist he help. Now she stared at him. How was he going to dig with only one arm?

"I may not be as fast as a man with two arms, but I can dig," he said, a hint of annoyance in his voice.

Elisabeth looked away but pointed toward the horse and cow stalls. Once Stefan returned with a spade, she directed him to start at the other end of the bed she was turning. She couldn't help but watch him out of the corner of her eye. He used his good arm to throw the spade into the ground, and then his foot to drive it in deeper. Next, he pulled the handle back, lifting the soil, then bent forward, tucked the top of the handle under his amputated arm, grabbed the handle halfway down with his hand, and then leveraged the spade the rest of the way out of the soil and turned it over. He returned to his beginning position and threw the spade back into the soil.

"Any sign of Maria's magazine when you returned home?"

The question eased the awkwardness of the situation.

"Not yet," Elisabeth answered, her eyes returning to her own work. "Anna's been angry at me since yesterday, because I won't let her help Mammi design new shoes. Mammi doesn't want to design new shoes, anyway, but still! Anna keeps insisting and I keep having to say no. Maybe she took it out of spite and won't tell me. Luki has no interest in these new shoes, so it can't be him. Rosina says she didn't take it, but she was so in love with what we saw that maybe she stole it just so she could look at it."

Stefan turned more soil over and then straightened up. "I've been thinking about what you said about Luki out on the *salasch*. Maybe Luki did take it," he suggested. "He's the only boy in the house. If everyone's so excited about these new designs, maybe he didn't want to feel left out." He threw the spade into the dirt again.

Elisabeth rested her hands and chin on the top of her spade for a moment. "I hadn't thought of that," she said. "Do you think he really feels like that?"

"He must. I certainly feel left out with this." He indicated his missing arm. "He has no one to show him how to play cards, or how to use the tools. I know your mother is helping him learn your father's trade, which is admirable, but from what I've seen—and please forgive me for saying so—he has no men to show him how to be a man."

Stefan returned to his digging, and Elisabeth did the same: she didn't want him to think she was leaving all the work to him. Judging by his grunts and his heavy breathing, it took him more effort to dig than it did her.

"Elisabeth!" The most welcome voice in the world...but not today. Elisabeth beckoned to Maria to come into the yard, but she worried about what Maria might think of Stefan's help. A look of surprise flashed across Maria's face when she spotted him.

"I should check on the animals and make sure they have enough hay for the night," Stefan said. He doffed his cap and left the girls alone.

Maria's face filled with curiosity and expectation. "Lissika," she whispered. "You have to tell me why he's here."

Elisabeth's cheeks flushed and she giggled. What was it about him that made her this nervous?

"Do you like him?"

Was that what this feeling was? Elisabeth had to admit that the first answer that sprang to mind was yes. But she didn't want to say that. As much as Elisabeth cherished Maria, she knew not every confidence would stay with Maria.

"He promised to help us out," she said matter-of-factly. "He's having a hard time finding work because of his arm. He hopes that if people see him helping us out they might trust him to hire him."

"By seeing him help in your kitchen garden?" The look on Maria's face told Elisabeth she didn't believe her answer.

"But I'm sure you're not here to spy on me," Elisabeth said with a smile.

Maria's shoulders dropped. "I'll have to ask you again another time. But no, I actually came here to see if you've found my magazine yet."

Elisabeth sighed and shook her head. "I've asked everyone, but no one will admit to taking it. I'm really sorry. I know how special that magazine is to you. I haven't stopped looking yet—I'm certain you're right and that it's here somewhere, but I can't even think where anyone would hide it."

The look of disappointment on Maria's face tugged at Elisabeth's heart. That someone in her family would violate the seventh commandment—*Thou shalt not steal*— humiliated her.

Maria tightened the knot under her white headscarf. "I know you're trying. I do hope you find it. The cable ferry is operating again, so my parents are going to take me to Arad for a few days. My father has to wait on a few parts being made by your cousin and Smith Konrad, so while he waits he can take a few days off. I was hoping to bring the magazine with me so I can look for some of that elegant clothing."

Smith Konrad was the villagers' name for Konrad-Bátschi. Georg and his father were repairing a few parts for the Haibach mill. The Haibachs also had day labourers—including Stefan's parents, Elisabeth now knew—who would take care of the family's *salasch*, home garden, and animals in their absence.

"I'm so sorry," Elisabeth said, a knot of embarrassment forming in her stomach. "I promise to keep looking."

Maria and Elisabeth kissed on both cheeks. Maria waved as she headed back to her house.

Stefan returned a few moments later, as though he had waited until Maria left. "Animals are all fed!" he announced.

Elisabeth smiled in acknowledgement but couldn't shake the feeling that she was failing her best friend.

CHAPTER SEVEN

It was Friday, and still no photo. Juliana wasn't going to search the dungeon again by herself, she had no excuse to look in the garage (nor any inclination to, since it wasn't heated), and Opa's room had turned up nothing except a lot of concern on Mom's part.

She rang the doorbell at the Morgan home.

"Juliana?" Aunt Anne said, rubbing her hands on a tea towel. "Shouldn't you be doing your own homework? Maybe practising a bit?"

Juliana had thought about that, too, but school and dance could wait. "I've got all weekend to do my homework," she said, "and I just practiced for an hour at home."

Aunt Anne looked doubtful. "You've been worried this whole time that you're...well...not up to par with your team's level. Are you sure an hour is enough?"

Juliana looked at the ground. Aunt Anne was right, but the only thing that really motivated Juliana right now was that photo.

"Something's on your mind, isn't it?" Aunt Anne said. "I've got six kids, Juliana. There's nothing you can surprise me with." Juliana followed her inside.

"In all honesty," Juliana said as she removed her winter boots, "with this move, my marks, Rachel's mom…I don't know. I just want to do something *fun* for a change. Besides, we got really high marks on the weekend, so maybe I'm not as bad as I thought I was. And if I can find this photo, then it would be a cool gift for Mom's birthday."

"I can't argue with that, can I?" Aunt Anne said and pointed up to Sophie's room.

Juliana raced up the stairs. "I'm here!" she announced and grabbed the doorknob.

"Wait!" a panicked Sophie said, and Juliana paused. But the door was open a crack and Juliana looked in. Sophie took something off her face, threw it in a drawer in her desk, and closed the drawer.

"Okay!" Sophie replied and turned away from the large monitor at her desk, a somewhat artificial smile on her face. "I didn't know you were coming, but I'm so glad you're here. Math is killing me so much it's not even funny."

Juliana returned her cousin's smile. She knew now that Sophie was hiding something from her, but Juliana sensed it wasn't her place to ask.

"Do you want help with your homework? We can even spend just fifteen minutes on it. I'm sure it'll help you."

Sophie shook her head. "I've got all weekend to do my homework."

Juliana plopped herself down on Sophie's bed. "Okay. We've looked almost everywhere in Opa's house. What if your mom really does have it but she's forgotten?"

Sophie playfully stroked her chin, as though she were trying to act like a real detective. "If I were my mother..." She dropped her hand. "Our house is huge, but Mom's really organized. Photo albums. But..." Sophie pointed to her eyes.

"Can you at least help me find the newer albums? At the very least we know this picture isn't black and white."

"Very Nancy Drew," Sophie said.

"Okay, who is that?"

The surprised look on Sophie's face told Juliana she was supposed to know the answer to this question. "How could you not read Nancy Drew when you were a kid? She's only the greatest girl detective in history!"

"I guess it's because I don't like mysteries." Juliana realized the irony of her statement and laughed. "But if we ever find this photo, then maybe I will!"

The girls headed downstairs to the reading nook in the Morgan household. Juliana loved it: two walls of books, three brightly coloured bean bags on the floor, and a matching two-seater couch against the third wall, with windows above it.

"Photo albums and scrapbooks are over there." Sophie pointed to some lower shelves loaded with tall books, some of them brown with gold embossing and others brightly coloured. Juliana grabbed a scrapbook and opened it and Sophie did the same.

"This one's colour," Sophie said.

"This one's black and white." Juliana put it back and took Sophie's find out of her hand. She paged back to the front.

"This one has Christmas photos," she explained. "And here's you..." Juliana stopped. Sophie looked about eight and she was reading a chapter book she'd just received, wrapping paper still on her lap. Should she describe this photo? Or not mention anything about it? What if Sophie suddenly became sad because Juliana had found a photo where she could obviously still see?

"What?" Sophie asked.

"Um..." What could she say?

Sophie crossed her arms. "It's a picture of me, isn't it?"

"Yeah..."

"Stop it. Just stop! Why does everyone have to treat me so differently? Rebecca with her stupid training ideas— 'How's she going to learn to ask for herself if we don't force her to at home?' Mom's friends with their stupid whispered comments. 'Maybe she just needs a stronger pair of glasses.' I'm sick of it! They talk about me like I don't have feelings. I don't need that!"

"I'm sorry...I didn't mean..."

"Did you tell your new friends to stop talking about your life before your move?"

Of course Juliana hadn't made any such request of Jasmine, Meghan, or Shawna. But she did need to act differently around Sophie, at least a little. As soon as they had arrived in Kitchener, Mom had made it clear that Sophie couldn't see everything, and Juliana had learned, for example, to say something like "That's funny" instead of just smiling or saying "Whatever" instead of just rolling her eyes. Laughing was okay—Sophie could see the rest of Juliana's face when she laughed and could also hear the laughter—but Juliana had to make sure she spoke more than she needed to around other friends. No one had to act differently around Juliana just because she'd moved.

Or did they?

Sophie dropped into a bean bag, interrupting Juliana's thoughts. "I'm sorry. I'm tired of everyone tiptoeing around me like I'm going to break. How else am I supposed to enjoy what you're seeing if you don't tell me about it?"

Juliana sighed, closed the album, and slumped against the back of her bean bag. She was trying really hard to figure out how to be helpful and nice, but she couldn't guess everything about Sophie either.

The girls sat quietly for a minute, neither saying

anything or moving. Juliana put the album back and selected one that looked older. She paged through it.

"This one looks like it's photos of Oma and Opa, our moms and a baby in their arms. That must be Uncle Peter." She flipped further ahead. "And I think this one's...yeah, it's your mom's birthday. Whoa!" She giggled and Sophie asked why. "I'm sorry—my mom's got the look of a killer on her face. I think she's jealous your mom gets to blow out the candles on her cake." Sophie laughed a little, too, now. Juliana checked the last page, and those photos were still too early to be of Mom dressed like a stuffed animal.

"You asked about my move," Juliana said, replacing the album. "My first thought was that no one has to treat me differently. But now I think you're right. Maybe we're kind of the same like that. People keep talking about different places and stuff, and I don't know what they mean and I have to keep saying that I'm new here. Then there are times when they mention some local place, and I know where it is, but they explain it to me anyways. I mean, I know it's not the same as, you know, losing your eyesight, but it's still annoying."

Sophie uncrossed her arms. "Yeah. And then people ask me if I've tried some cure-all herbal remedy, because their friend's friend's cousin's friend's sister's grandmother's cousin tried it and it worked, or something stupid like that."

Juliana burst out laughing. "Seriously? I always get

asked if I know so-and-so from Calgary. We've got over a million people living there!"

The girls laughed some more and the tension between them relaxed.

But Juliana knew in one sense their situations were very different: she would eventually learn her way around town, whereas Sophie would eventually lose most of her sight. But as far as how other people treated them, it felt almost the same. For now, anyway.

Juliana pulled out another album and was excited to see that it looked like it was from the same time period as the dance photo. She flipped through it, describing to Sophie what she saw. By the end, though, no embarrassing photo of Mom had been found.

"I guess it's at Opa's house," Juliana said.

"I guess."

Both girls slouched in their bean bags. This search was a lot harder than Juliana had thought it would be.

JULIANA'S LEG KEPT SHAKING.

"Can you stop that?" Jasmine asked.

Juliana placed her elbow on it and then propped her chin up on top to hold the bouncing leg down, but then her other leg started.

"What are you so nervous about?" Mackenzie asked, staring at Juliana's other leg.

Miss Denise clicked on her mouse a few times.

"Judges' comments," Juliana replied.

Mackenzie rolled her eyes. "They're usually just stupid, anyway."

"Mackenzie," Miss Denise warned. "The point of listening to these is precisely to learn what's important to listen to and what you should ignore. When I was your age, the judges gave us their comments in front of everyone. You learned to deal with it. You kids have it way too easy."

Mackenzie crossed her arms. "She says that all the time," she muttered under her breath.

Miss Denise picked up her remote and stood back from the computer. The team watched as a video of the tap group's routine played.

"This first comment is from JX," Miss Denise said. JX was the hip-hop judge on the panel.

"Bang-up job on the opening," said a deep, smooth, male voice on the video. "Yup...yup. Bam! Incredible! You guys look great."

"I'm not a guy," Mackenzie said. Everyone ignored her.

"Oh...dancer upstage isn't quite with the others. She looks a little uncertain, not quite in sync. Is she new to the studio? If so, welcome! You chose a really good one to join. Boom! You guys nailed that riff combo!"

But Juliana barely heard the compliment. She was still

stuck at the comment about the new girl. She was the "dancer upstage."

Jasmine gave her a friendly pat on the shoulder. "You only learned this two months ago," she said. *They do treat me differently because I'm new*, Juliana thought. If she'd been with the team for years, the comment would've been, "You had a bad day. Don't worry about it."

"Ooooh, baby, that turn sequence. Boom! Nailed it! Uh-huh...uh-huh...Dancer moving from upstage left to down-stage right is on the wrong foot."

Juliana buried her face in her hands. That was her again.

"Juliana," Miss Denise said, and Juliana looked up. "Take note of the error and decide how you're going to incorporate it into your practice. Then move on. Feeling embarrassed isn't going to make you a better dancer."

Right now, nothing is going to make me a better dancer, she thought, though in her heart she knew that wasn't true.

"Dancer moving downstage left, excellent footwork."

Savannah patted Mackenzie—the one with the excellent footwork—on the back. Mackenzie smiled. Juliana looked away.

As the comments continued, Juliana was certain she was the only one called out so often. Didn't the judge recognize he was criticizing the same one the entire time? *I mean, how can he not see that? I'm the worst one...my leg didn't go high enough there. Ugh!*

Juliana promised herself to practise harder. *I can't search for that photo anymore. My team needs me and I need to up my game.* She also thought about Aunt Anne's comments, that Juliana should practise more and that Sophie needed to work on her math. Juliana didn't want to get Sophie in trouble—she was obviously dealing with a lot more than Juliana knew about—and she also didn't want to be the cause for her team getting only high golds and golds next time. *Without me, they probably would've gotten all platinum,* she thought.

Juliana would have to think up of another birthday gift for Mom. But what would make her as happy as that photo?

IT WAS ALREADY TEN O'CLOCK AT NIGHT, BUT WHEN JULIANA'S phone rang, she squealed. Rachel! Their friendship hadn't been the same since Rachel's mom had died. As much as Juliana had tried to help Rachel get through the funeral and the move to her dad's house, the tragedy showed both girls just how hard it was to maintain a friendship from halfway across the country. They didn't even text or call each other every day anymore.

But that didn't mean Juliana wouldn't be thrilled when Rachel called. "Hey!" Juliana said as she dropped on to her bed. "How are things?"

"We sold our old house, Mom's and mine," Rachel said. "But they're letting me finish the school year at our school, so at least that's good."

Juliana didn't know what to say, but she remembered advice from Shawna, one of her new friends at school here. Shawna had lost her father to cancer a few years before. She'd told Juliana that when someone loses a person who's close to them, it was best to say as little as possible and just to listen.

"Well, I guess, you know, that is good, like you said," Juliana replied. The following pause told her she needed to say something more, so she did her best to make sure it was supportive. "What else is going on?" She cringed at her own question: Hopefully Rachel wouldn't interpret it as a suggestion to change the subject.

"Well, Dad has me seeing a counsellor. Jules, I don't know what I'm supposed to talk about. Dad says it'll help me, but, I mean, Mom died. Life sucks. What else do you say?"

"I don't know," Juliana replied, not wanting to offer up any stories or anything. She still had both her parents, her family had grown by ten once she'd moved here, and she'd never been to a funeral before. What could she say?

"Anyways...I'm tired of talking about it," Rachel said and Juliana took note. "I mean, everyone looks at me now like I'm Little Orphan Annie from the musical or something like that and need to be saved by Daddy Warbucks.

It's gotten to the point where I even wake up singing 'Tomorrow' in my head."

Besides the fact that Rachel did not have red, curly hair like Annie in the musical, she also didn't come from a horrible orphanage, like Annie did. But so far as Juliana knew, no one else on her old dance team had lost a parent. In that way, Rachel stood out just as much as Annie's red hair and freckled face did.

Rachel then changed the subject. "I saw online that you had your first competition with the new team? Your costumes looked awesome. How was it?"

Juliana sighed. "Good and not so good." She twirled her hair around her finger.

"What happened?"

Juliana told her about the high scores and how amazing she had felt when they had arrived home. When she mentioned her special award for having the most tap screws with her, Rachel burst out laughing. "Oh my god, that is so you!"

That is so me, she thought, laughing just as loudly.

"Juliana!" Mom called through her door. "A little quiet, please! I've got an early morning tomorrow!"

"Sorry, Mom!" she yelled back. Then she caught herself. Should she have said "Mom"? Would that make Rachel sad again? She thought about what Sophie had said, about how people treat you differently because you're somehow different, and then what Rachel had said a few minutes ago. Having your mom killed by a drunk driver definitely makes you different.

"Say hi to her for me," Rachel said, a touch of sadness in her voice. Juliana relayed the message, Mom returned it, and Juliana passed that on, too.

Rachel returned to their conversation, in a happier mood. "But it sounds like you did awesome!" she said.

"Yeah, but then the judges kept singling me out for a bunch of mistakes."

"Ouch. But you were one of the best at our studio. What happened?"

Juliana sighed again. "I moved." Moments like these left her wondering if she'd ever fit in. She wasn't one of the gang back in Calgary anymore, despite trying to jump in on conversations online. Although her team here accepted her, Juliana had only known them for two months, hardly long enough to feel that bond she felt with her old team. She felt the same at school. Meghan and Shawna were nice to hang out with, but they had known each other since grade school. Juliana could tell by some of their glances that they knew they were thinking the same thing. It wasn't anything mean but she still felt left out.

"Jules, you've been working your butt off since you moved. I think you've got to give yourself some credit for that."

Juliana could always count on Rachel to cheer her up.

"Thanks, but I've got a long way to go before I get as good as everyone else."

"Then get practising."

Juliana knew Rachel was right. *But that photo*...she thought.

CHAPTER EIGHT

The following morning, after Elisabeth had sent Luki and Anna off to school, she and Rosina began turning the garden beds. Stefan had helped Elisabeth spread dung on all the beds after they'd finished turning one of them, so all she and Rosina had to do was turn the soil. Unfortunately, though, Rosina was too small to use a spade, so she sat on an old blanket and used a trowel.

"What's Tata doing right now?" Rosina asked.

How was Elisabeth supposed to know the answer to that? "I don't know. Probably working."

"What does he do?"

"He makes cigars." At Rosina's confused look, Elisabeth explained further. "Some of the men here smoke them.

They're like cigarettes, but they're brown, bigger, and they stink."

Rosina thought for a moment. "Like what Georg puts in his mouth? Those big brown things and not the small white ones? He smokes the white ones."

Elisabeth nodded and Rosina wrinkled her nose. "The brown ones smell like a skunk," she said. Elisabeth laughed.

Both girls continued digging and Elisabeth thought now was a good time to ask again about the magazine. Thinking back to her studies, she chose to start with the commandments. *Maybe a little push from God will help me*, she thought.

"Rosina, do you understand the eighth commandment? It says, 'Thou shalt not bear false witness against thy neighbour.'"

Rosina nodded, which surprised Elisabeth. She had honestly expected her to say no. But a feeling in her stomach told her something wasn't right.

"All right, then. What does it mean?"

"I don't know."

Elisabeth sighed. "Then why did you say you did?"

Rosina shoved the trowel into the earth and grimaced at a worm she pulled up. "Because I thought I was supposed to."

Elisabeth looked up at the sky. *Why?* she asked Jesus. Then to her sister she said, "It means you shouldn't tell lies about other people. If you do, God will punish you severely."

Rosina froze. "How?"

Elisabeth recited from Martin Luther's *Small Catechism*, the book she had been fervently memorizing in preparation for her confirmation on Palm Sunday: "God threatens to punish all that transgress these commandments. Therefore we should fear His wrath, and not act contrary to them. But He promises grace and every blessing to all that keep these commandments. Therefore we should also love and trust in Him, and willingly do according to His commandments." In her imagination, Elisabeth patted herself on the back for her recitation.

But Rosina's face wrinkled in confusion. "What does all that mean?"

Elisabeth had never tried to explain what Luther had meant. She struggled to find words that Rosina would understand. "Martin Luther says that...God threatens to punish anyone...who doesn't listen to Him. But if you listen to God...He'll be nice to you." Another imaginary pat on the back: Rosina looked like she understood.

"But what happens when you don't listen to God?" Rosina asked.

Elisabeth thought for a moment—she wanted to give her sister an honest answer, because that's what Jesus would want from her. But she had to admit, she wasn't entirely sure. After some thought, she shrugged and said, "I suppose you'll burn in hell."

"Oh." Rosina shifted her position and then dug a little more with her trowel. "Does that hurt?"

Elisabeth placed her forehead on the end of her shovel's shaft. Was it really this hard to raise children? She raised her head and drove the shovel into the earth. "All I'm saying is that it's wrong to tell lies about other people."

"So I can tell lies about myself?"

Elisabeth couldn't wait for Rosina to start school.

"Fine. Do you know what happened to Maria's magazine?"

"No."

"Even though you know God will punish you if you're lying? God will bless you with nice...things...if you tell the truth."

Rosina's eyes lit up. Was she going to tell Elisabeth now what had happened to the magazine?

"Does that mean if I say I did it, that God will give me presents, even if I didn't take it? Or is that lying?"

Elisabeth dropped her forehead onto the shaft of her shovel again and repeated her question to Jesus: *Why?*

SEVERAL HOURS LATER, ELISABETH AND ROSINA WERE INSIDE, dusting the back room. They had completed two more beds in the garden, although Elisabeth had done most of the work. Someone knocked at the door. The sisters put their dusters down and went to answer it. Before Elisabeth could open the door fully, Rosina bolted out of the kitchen and ran into the front room.

"Georg," Elisabeth said, surprised. Georg knew Mammi didn't like him coming here: he had even acknowledged it himself once when he'd had a fit in public and Elisabeth had insisted that he and Eva rest in her home. He knew that Mammi despised him, and why. "Come in."

Georg stepped inside. He removed his hat but held it in his hand instead of giving it to Elisabeth.

"I can take your coat," she offered.

He shook his head. "I won't stay long."

Movement in the front room caught their attention, and Elisabeth almost covered her eyes in disbelief. Rosina was climbing under the table, clutching her doll as though it were her last day on earth.

Jesus, I promise to talk to Rosina about this later, but please, PLEASE don't let her embarrass me again. At least not today.

"May I speak with Lissa-Néni? Samuel and I have a proposition for her."

Elisabeth nodded. "I'll be right back. Please, if you want to, have a seat...um...maybe in the kitchen?"

"I'm fine, thank you," Georg said.

Elisabeth looked at both of them: Rosina's face full of

fear, Georg's completely still. She hurried to the workshop and returned a few minutes later with Mammi.

Mammi planted her hands on her hips, her gaze digging into Georg's expressionless face. "What is so important that you have to interrupt me?"

Mammi's anger toward Georg originated when both were children. Four years younger than Mammi, Georg had mocked her and her friends on their daily walk home after he had started school. Mammi was not the only one he behaved so poorly toward, of course. As Georg grew, Mammi had told Elisabeth, it had gotten worse. He and his friends would try to lift girls' skirts, pick fights with the boys, and throw insults at the adults. Very few stood up to him because Konrad-Bátschi would always protect him. Mammi had said that by the time he was a *großbube*, Georg was almost twice the size of any grown man and could win almost any fight.

But Mammi's anger toward her nephew had entrenched itself deep inside her during the war: After declaring that Mammi's first brother, Adam-Bátschi, had died in the war because he was of "poor stock," as Mammi had told Elisabeth, Georg had promised to protect Andreas-Bátschi, another one of Mammi's brothers, on the front. To everyone's surprise, the two men became close friends. Sadly, Georg had returned from the war and Andreas-Bátschi had not. Although Elisabeth knew Georg couldn't have prevented his friend's death—their commanding officer had separated them during battle—she also understood Mammi's anger toward him. In Mammi's mind, a promise was a promise. However, Elisabeth hoped that Mammi would eventually see in Georg what she saw.

Georg, too, skipped the niceties. "Samuel and I wish to look after your land this season."

Mammi drew her lips into a thin line. "We need the full harvest to feed us."

Customarily, if someone else looked after a family's land, that person was paid in food from the harvest and often meat from the family's animals. The arrangement was called sharecropping. A normal sharecropping arrangement meant about half of the harvest went to the farmer.

But with Tata gone, what other choice do we have? Elisabeth thought. *If Georg can take care of our fields, we need his help. So why is Mammi refusing?*

Georg stood firm, unmoved by Mammi's anger. "Lissa-Néni, with my uncle gone, you have neither a man to feed nor help you. Samuel and I ask for nothing. It will not repay the debt—"

"You can never repay your debt to me or my family," Mammi interrupted.

Never? Elisabeth thought. *Jesus, make her change her mind!*

Georg lowered his gaze. "I couldn't help my first wife

and child, and I failed your brother. He was a good man. He didn't deserve..." He wrung his hands together, and Elisabeth worried another fit might overcome him. To her relief, he continued. "I can only help your family." Elisabeth's heart broke. Georg hadn't learned of the deaths of his first wife and child until he had returned. Stefan had told Elisabeth once that this was part of the reason for Georg's nightmares. Couldn't Mammi see his regret through her anger? If Georg was Jesus's answer to Elisabeth's prayers, why was Mammi refusing?

Georg relaxed his hands. "Elisabeth would still need to help once each week, but I would take her there myself with your horse and wagon. I would have her back by sundown."

"What about your father?" Mammi said.

"I will help him, of course, but he can still manage much of the workshop on his own."

Now Mammi looked doubtful. "I know your father. I don't believe he would approve of your offer."

"The land is no longer his. It's none of his concern."

"But his workshop is still not yours."

Mammi, covered from head to toe in dark blue and brown, with only her face and hands showing, stood like one of the pillars holding up the balcony in the church. She had always kept her distance from Konrad-Bátschi's family. Even when Susi, their youngest child, had married last month, Mammi had sent Elisabeth and Anna to help, with instructions to pass on her regrets. Konrad-Bátschi and Margarethe-Néni looked down on Elisabeth's family and showed their disdain any time they could.

Mammi had many reasons to despise not only Georg but his whole family. *But we have to move on*, Elisabeth thought. *We need their help.*

"No," Mammi said. "My answer is firm. We will find a way to manage our land without your family's help."

"Mammi," Elisabeth said. "Please reconsider. We can't—"

Anger flashed in Mammi's eyes. "I said no!" Elisabeth jumped at Mammi's outburst, but Georg didn't flinch. "I will not accept help from your father's family."

Georg nodded, placed his hat back on his head, and reached for the doorknob. "Our offer still stands and always will." He tipped his hat to both of them and then left, softly closing the door behind him.

Elisabeth turned to her mother, anger bursting out. "Why would you turn down such a generous offer? I don't know how we're going to make it through this season!"

Mammi slapped Elisabeth hard on the cheek. "If you ever talk to me like that again, you will kneel in that box of corn kernels for an hour! What do you expect to happen, Elisabeth? That no one will notice that a crazy man is helping us? They'll stop bringing me their shoes as fast as God banished Lucifer. Where do you want us to earn our extra money? Or should we end up like Stefan's family—

day labourers who live hand to mouth? Do you want that to happen?"

Mammi didn't wait for an answer, storming out of the house and slamming the door behind her.

Elisabeth placed a hand on her burning cheek and looked up to Jesus on His crucifix on the wall. Tears welled in her eyes. *Why can't You make her see that this is the right answer?*

"I don't understand," Rosina's quiet voice said, surprising Elisabeth, who had forgotten her sister was there. "Georg offered Mammi help, and Mammi said no."

Elisabeth wiped her eyes dry. She couldn't explain all of this to Rosina. "I'll tell you when you're older," she said.

Rosina crossed her arms and stomped back in the front room, where she picked up her knitting project. "I hate when everyone tells me that!"

"But I need help with the back room..." Elisabeth started and then dropped it. She also needed some time alone to try to simmer down or she'd explode at Anna and Luki when they returned from school.

She strode into the back room, picked up her duster, and continued with her chores.

CHAPTER NINE

"I feel so left out here," Brian said as he moved his piece around the game board. He glanced at each of the men sitting around the table as he said their names. "Peter, Paul, Phil, and...Brian. I mean, even your dad's name is Peter," he said to the Schuhmacher siblings. "Everyone else's name starts with *p*."

Juliana laughed. She had to admit it was weird.

"Hey!" Uncle Peter said and gave Brian a good punch in the shoulder: Brian had just knocked out one of his pieces.

Uncle Peter's trip to France had been delayed so he had invited everyone over to his place for a game of *Frustration* and store-bought snacks. Dad had commented on the way there that Uncle Peter was known as a "non-cook." "He'd probably burn the place down if he turned on his stove," Dad had said in the car.

Uncle Peter's condo fit his personality: loud and cheerful with white walls, brightly coloured furniture, and immense, abstract paintings. Music from the '80s was playing in the background. The chorus was something like, "We are the world...we are the children."

"Juliana, your turn!" Uncle Peter said. "And if you can get Brian out for me, I'll be forever grateful." He flashed his smile.

Juliana slammed her hand onto the plastic dome that covered the die. "A six!" She pulled one of her pieces out of its corner and placed it on the board. She hit the dome again. Her shoulders drooped. A two. Should she move this piece or one farther ahead on the *Frustration* board? The second one was in danger of being sacrificed to Dad's piece, which was four spots behind her.

She moved the new piece. What were the chances Dad would get a four?

"You know," Uncle Peter said, "I had such a crush on Huey when I was a kid."

Who was Huey?

"Nope, Paul Simon," Brian said. The name sounded familiar, but that was all Juliana knew.

"Well, I'm certainly no Paul Simon," Dad said, wiggling his belly. Juliana cringed and Dad smiled. "I can sing—"

"No," Juliana said. "You can't." Everyone laughed. Why did dads do this? Rachel's father embarrassed her all the time in front of their friends. Once, he had tried pinning one of Rachel's hairpieces to his head and had attempted pirouettes. The adults had roared with laughter but the kids had looked in the other direction. Rachel's cheeks turned redder than her stage-makeup blush.

"Better watch out, Jules," Dad said, "I'm coming for you!"

When Uncle Peter had brought the game off his shelf, Juliana was amazed by how pristine the box looked. Everyone she knew—her parents included—had board games that looked ready for a garage sale. But this one had its own shelf, surrounded by figurines standing at attention, guarding the game.

Nooo! Dad had popped a four on the die.

"That is so not fair!" Juliana exclaimed as Dad gave her an evil grin and knocked her piece off its space. "No wonder it's called *Frustration*."

"In German," Uncle Peter said, "it's called *mensch ärgere dich nicht*. 'Dude, don't get annoyed.'"

"*Mensch* does not mean dude," Brian said. "I don't know a lot of German, but I know that much."

"No," Uncle Peter said, "but we wouldn't say, 'Person, don't get annoyed.' But I'm not young anymore. Juliana, would you say 'dude'?"

"Uh..."

"I gotcha!" Dean shouted from the sofa. Juliana looked over, and all her cousins—except Sophie—were playing vintage Pac-Man. Sophie sat in an arm chair all by herself.

Juliana had wanted to go over to her, but she'd been pulled into this game.

"Are you sure you don't want to play?" Rebecca offered the controller to Sophie.

"You know I can't see the screen."

Rebecca pulled the controller away. "If you'd wear your glasses, you could be playing with us."

Glasses? What glasses? Sophie had never mentioned anything about glasses. *Or was that what she'd shoved in her drawer?* Juliana wondered. Half the world had glasses. *Even Mom needs glasses for reading*, she thought. *So does Aunt Anne. What's the big deal?* Juliana would ask her about it, but not in front of her family.

"Hey, Sophie," she called over. Sophie perked up. "Any luck with that picture?"

Sophie shook her head. "Mom's sure she doesn't have it."

Aunt Anne was picking up Opa from the airport this evening, so she wasn't there, and Mom was at work. Uncle Peter lived in Uptown Waterloo, which was really downtown Waterloo, but anytime Juliana called it that, she got corrected: downtown Kitchener and Uptown Waterloo. Mom had said it was because both downtowns were on King Street, and Waterloo lay north of Kitchener. Dad had said it was just marketing.

"Are you guys still looking for that photo?" Uncle Peter

asked. Sophie walked over to the table to join the conversation.

"Opa told me once he was sure it's around, but we haven't been able to find it yet," Juliana said.

"You know how Opa's memory is," Uncle Peter said.

"I know, but he does remember a lot, too."

"You sure you don't remember something?" Uncle Phillip asked Uncle Peter. "Annie told me about it, and she thinks Katy got rid of it."

Juliana popped the die. A six! "Ha!" she said to Dad and pulled her piece out of the corner again.

"Wow, you've got all the luck," Dad said.

Uncle Peter flashed a huge smile. "That's why I love this game. You never know what'll happen. Like in real life." He gave Brian the cheesiest smile and a peck on the cheek.

"Seriously?" Juliana asked. "There are kids here."

Brian looked angry and hurt.

"She can't stand it when *any* adults she knows kiss," Dad explained. "When Katy comes, I'll show you what I mean."

Juliana grimaced. The last thing she wanted was to see her parents give each other noisy kisses. "*Ew!* Sophie! *Ew,* right?"

Sophie shuddered. "Disgusting!"

Everyone laughed, including Brian.

"We were going to try the garage," Sophie added.

"Don't bother," Dad said. "We've got so many boxes in there. You'll never get past them."

Juliana folded her arms across her chest and stared at her lap. Dad rubbed her briefly on her back. "It was a really nice thought, though. I'm sure Mom'll be happy to know you tried to find it."

Sophie interjected. "But she's sure Opa's sure. We haven't looked everywhere, so maybe it's still in the house somewhere."

Brian asked Uncle Peter, "Actually, didn't you tell me once that your mother always checked the garbage? How could Katy have thrown it out?"

"You're right," Dad said. "Now that you mention it, Katy's told me that, too. Their mom checked their school bags all the time."

Uncle Phillip snapped his fingers. "Yeah—Annie's mentioned that, too. Katy couldn't have gotten rid of it."

"Your mom couldn't throw anything out, wasn't that it?" Brian asked Uncle Peter.

Uncle Peter shook his head. "The Second World War never fully left her, even though she was only two when it was over. I guess her parents were somehow really traumatized by it and then the Communist dictatorship that followed."

Uncle Peter might as well have been speaking German again. Juliana had no idea what he meant.

"Tata was never as strict about throwing things out,"

Uncle Peter continued, "but Modr would even find a use for old underwear. Don't ask me what it was. But in my teens, I'd throw out an old pair, and the next day, they were no longer in the garbage."

Juliana and Sophie cringed again.

"I learned early on to never go into the cellar," Uncle Peter said. "It was her 'special place.'" He used air quotes.

That explained all the mason jars and lids, but the encyclopedias? They were definitely Opa's. Or maybe he had put them in there after she had died?

The phone on the wall rang and Uncle Peter answered it.

"Annie and Tata are here!" he announced.

Juliana felt giddy. Even though she and her parents had only been living with Opa for a short time, she had missed his presence this past week. On the days she got home from school and Mom and Dad were at work, not even Opa had been there all week to greet her. He wasn't home all the time, but an entire week without him had made the small bungalow feel empty.

Game-playing continued for another two minutes. Then Aunt Anne and Opa knocked on the door and Uncle Peter opened it. Opa stood there, tanned and in a Hawaiian shirt and tan-coloured slacks. He looked shocked upon seeing everyone and Juliana worried his dementia was to blame. But a moment later, she knew it wasn't.

"Besides Katy, the whole family's here?" His face grew

into such a big smile that Juliana could see where Uncle Peter had gotten his from.

"I'm right behind you, Tata," Mom said, standing in the hallway. "My assistant manager said he'd lock up."

Opa beamed. "My entire family is here?"

Juliana looked around the room. They were all here, and this was her family, too, now. She had to admit, the more she got to know everyone, the more she could accept them as family. Back in Calgary, she'd always felt a little left out because so many of her friends had had other family in the city, and if not there, then in Edmonton, Red Deer, or in any of the towns that lay between the major cities in the province. When she had first arrived in Kitchener at Christmas, all the new faces had overwhelmed her, which was why she'd escaped to that dungeon in the first place where she'd discovered Omama's book of drawings. But since then, this "new" family had grown on her, helped her when she got down on herself, and—she glanced over at Sophie —was actually fun to be around.

As Opa went to all his grandchildren and ruffled their hair or squeezed their shoulder, Juliana knew she'd have to wait until later to ask him about the photo again.

But that was okay. For now, she was going to enjoy her family, too.

"AND SO I SPILLED THE WATER ON KARL," OPA SAID TO Juliana with a grin. "You should have seen him try to jump! His knees were so bad he couldn't get up fast enough!" Juliana laughed. What was it about old people and their bodies? Every complaint and joke seemed to be about them. "He stopped teasing me about the way I walk after that," Opa said, finishing his story. "He was calling it the 'Schuhmacher Shuffle.'"

Juliana giggled. That actually described Opa's walk perfectly.

Opa and Juliana were sitting on the orange couch in the living room, the one that was so old it had a board underneath it so you didn't sink into its base. After what Juliana had heard about Oma earlier in the evening, she wondered if Opa had kept this couch because he didn't want to throw it away. Why else keep a couch this broken?

"What did you do while I was away? Did you look at any of your Omama's drawings?" Opa asked. "I thought about you in Cuba. I missed talking to you about her."

Juliana's heart melted. "No," she replied. "I've been so busy with school, and dance, and finding that photo you told me about."

Opa turned to face her. "What photo?"

"The one you told me about before you left? Of Mom in some kind of embarrassing, fuzzy costume?"

Opa looked like he was searching his memory and

eventually shook his head. "No, I didn't say anything like that."

"But you told me about it. I know you did." *Or am I the one making things up now?* she asked herself. On the one hand, no one believed the photo existed. On the other, they couldn't figure out how it could have disappeared given Oma's unwillingness to throw away anything.

Mom's quick footsteps came down the hallway, where the bedrooms were, and she appeared in the doorway to the living room. "Tata, we need to talk," she said.

"Uh, oh," Opa said to Juliana. "Looks like I'm in trouble." He pushed himself off the couch.

Mom's face immediately relaxed. "Sorry. I didn't mean it like that."

"Are you going to explain my new closet to me?"

Mom smiled. "It was actually Juliana's idea. Then you don't have to worry about tripping over your clothes."

Opa turned to face Juliana and pointed to his head. "You're smart like a fox. I found all my clothes in it when we got back from Uncle Peter's."

Mom led Opa to the basement. Juliana knew Mom had to talk to him about more than his clothing, and that left a queasy knot in her stomach. She was only beginning to get to know Opa and his memory was already slipping. His dementia must have been much harder on Mom.

I wonder how Mom feels about everything, she thought. Mom had been working so hard and missing out on so much fun with the family that that photo might make her happy—even just for a little while. The surprise birthday party was in exactly one week. Juliana could spend a few more hours searching for it.

I guess the only way to find out is to look in the dungeon and the garage again, Juliana thought as she walked to her room. Juliana had checked the garage earlier that morning when she had grabbed some salt for sprinkling on the driveway outside. There was an opening between the boxes and Opa's workbench, but it was too small for her to look inside.

She flicked on the light to her bedroom and then realized that Sophie was possibly still small enough to fit through. Sophie might not be able to see everything, but she might remember or be able to feel a secret hiding spot or something.

"It's worth a try," she said to herself.

CHAPTER TEN

lthough the days were beginning to get longer, with April approaching, darkness still fell early. The Schuhmachers had several lanterns placed on the table in the front room so the girls could work on their handicrafts in the evenings. Luki was trying to build a house of cards.

"You know," Elisabeth said as she hemmed one of Anna's old dresses for Rosina, "I already know someone else besides Maria who would buy nicer shoes from Mammi if she could make them. But without that magazine, there's nothing she can follow."

Anna, busy with embroidering a handkerchief for Mammi, said, "You can draw, and you've seen the magazine a few times. Draw Mammi something."

Did this mean Anna had stolen it? Elisabeth needed to press further.

"My memory isn't good enough to draw those shoes in the same amount of detail," she said. "If Mammi had those pictures, I could copy them and she could start."

"But Mammi doesn't want to," Luki said. "She doesn't want to learn anything new. And making shoes is already hard."

"But it would be so much fun to decorate them!" Rosina said. She had succeeded with her fifth row of knitting and now worked away at the sixth one.

Elisabeth couldn't let it rest. "But don't you all understand? If we can help Mammi create a design that's not too difficult for her, then she can charge more. We could replace our roof sooner and hire farmhands to help with our land. Who knows? Maybe Tata could even come home sooner. But we need that magazine."

Anna eyed her piece of work. "First of all, Rosina said Georg offered to help. So, he should do that. The *salasch* is far away, and I won't have to speak to him." Elisabeth's blood began to boil. "Second, I won't have time to help Mammi because I'll be busy in the house. That's what you said. Luki doesn't want to help, and Rosina's too young."

"I am not!"

"Are too!"

"Am not!"

The house door opened and a cool evening draft shot through the front room, wrapping itself around the siblings' ankles. Mammi had come in to retire for the day. Because of the midwife's instructions that Mammi nap in the afternoon, she now worked late into the evening instead of joining her family in the front room to sew or weave.

"Think about it," Elisabeth said to them, seething. "For all our sakes."

She placed her sewing on the table, prayed to Jesus to help her calm down, and went to the kitchen to see if Mammi needed any help.

Mammi untied her brown headscarf from under her chin and passed it to Elisabeth, along with the several shawls she had wrapped around her shoulders. She said not a word.

When Mammi entered the front room, the lanterns threw shadows on her face, highlighting the shallow, tired wrinkles that outlined her features.

"You look tired," Elisabeth said.

"I can help you decorate the shoes!" Rosina said, not paying one moment's attention to Mammi's exhaustion. Elisabeth shot her a look but not before Mammi scolded her.

"I'm tired," she said through clenched teeth. "I neither have the time nor the desire to try something new."

"But—"

"That's enough!" All four children froze and a shiver

raced down Elisabeth's spine. "First Georg and now my own family!" Mammi yelled. She undid the tie under her *haube*, a white, plain bonnet that fitted close to the head and that only married women wore, set it on the table, and let down her braid.

"Get back to your work," Mammi said. Elisabeth's siblings returned to their activities. Elisabeth, though, continued watching Mammi as she undid her braid.

"I do not wish to hear it." Mammi watched herself in the looking glass as she began to brush out her waist-long hair.

But Elisabeth had learned over the past little while that sometimes even Mammi was wrong, and that sometimes the right thing to do was to tell her so. It was why Elisabeth had called the midwife after Mammi had been sick for at least a month. Of course, Mammi never liked being wrong, but Elisabeth knew deep down that she had to speak up again.

Elisabeth wiped her hands on her white apron to get rid of the sweat on her palms. "Maria and her mother would already order nicer shoes from you," she began. Out of the corner of her eye, she could see her siblings look up, apprehensive. They probably feared another of Mammi's outbursts. Elisabeth continued. "Eva would like such a pair, too. I know they're not the only ones who would order something different from our usual shoes, and because they're so nice, you could charge more for them."

Mammi turned to face Elisabeth, her lips drawn into their usual tight, unsmiling line. "Who will teach me how to make these? When will I have time to make them? And why should we even want fashionable shoes when the shoes we already wear are good enough?" Mammi continued brushing her hair, placing the brush at the top of her skull and pulling it all the way down to the tips of her hair.

Elisabeth spoke carefully. "If Georg and Samuel tend to our land, you will have time to learn."

"Georg only wants our family's land because he knows his father won't give him any," she said. "He wants me to trust him so he can convince me to sell it to him." She glared at Elisabeth. "And I won't." She opened a drawer in the wall unit, pulled out an old, woven cloth and her night-gown, and headed to the washing bowl in the kitchen. "I'm going to go wash myself," Mammi said. "The matter is closed."

Elisabeth couldn't let this rest. After the couple of times she had already been out to the farm, she knew that managing all that land, plus their small vineyard, the animals, and their kitchen garden was too much for a young family. Moreover, Elisabeth was certain Georg wanted nothing of the sort. After what he had said to Mammi earlier that day, Elisabeth believed he actually sought Mammi's forgiveness and that tending to her fami-ly's land in Tata's absence was part of that.

She followed Mammi into the kitchen. "He doesn't. He really wants to help us."

Mammi flashed Elisabeth an angry look. "The answer is no, on both conversations." Mammi picked up the empty water jug and took it outside to fill. "Collect some ash from the oven," she told Elisabeth as she closed the door behind her. Elisabeth retrieved a rag from the kitchen cabinet, opened the oven door, and collected some ash so Mammi could wash her hair. The heat from the oven warmed her face.

"We need help," Anna said. Elisabeth looked into the front room. Anna pleaded with her eyes. "It doesn't make sense that we can tend to everything without Tata here. Georg and Samuel are men. They can help us." Elisabeth smiled. Despite Anna's prickly personality, Elisabeth could count on her to give a logical suggestion to any problem. "I won't have time to do my homework if I have to help in the fields and the kitchen garden," she added. "Then Herr Blum will make me sit at the back."

Herr Blum, the teacher at Anna and Luki's school, had said several times how smart Anna was, and that it was too bad she was a girl. Otherwise, he would have tried to find a way for her to attend grade seven outside of Semlak so that she could go to secondary school afterwards. But a girl's position was to become a housewife, not a student. Still, so long as Anna enjoyed school and wanted to learn, Elisabeth knew she had to support that.

It was perhaps the one positive connection between the sisters.

"I can't learn how to make shoes if I have to help out there, too," Luki said. Elisabeth agreed with him. If Luki spent too much time working the land, he couldn't learn from Mammi. "But not the new shoes," he added. "I already have too much to learn." Elisabeth rolled her eyes.

"Georg scares me," Rosina said. "I don't want to help when he's helping. But otherwise he can help." The other two nodded. Elisabeth wished they could see past his still expressions, hulking build, and terrifying fits. *I suppose if I was their age, though, I would be scared of him, too*, she thought. But her siblings were right: their small family, with three young children—two of them in school—could not take care of everything.

Elisabeth placed the ash in a cloth, closed the oven door, and set the cloth next to the washing bowl. What would Tata do? She remembered how Mammi and Tata would sometimes shoo the children out of the room and close the door so they could talk about something. Would that work for Elisabeth, too?

Mammi returned from the well. Elisabeth had to try. She gave a quick nod to her siblings and closed the door between the kitchen and the front room.

Mammi placed the jug of water next to the washing bowl. "I said no." She held the cloth with ash over the jug and poured some of the water from the washing bowl into it to make a sort of tea she would use to rinse her hair. She leaned over the bowl and splashed water on her face.

"Look how tired you are," Elisabeth said. "And the others don't know what I know. When the baby comes, am I to look after it? Because if you do, there will be no one to make shoes. I don't know how to look after a baby. How can I do that, clean the house, take care of my siblings, tend the fields, and still cook? How are we going to handle all of this?"

Mammi's hands stopped for a moment but then she grabbed a cloth to dry her face. That she had paused signalled to Elisabeth that she had Mammi's attention. "You have always told us that God will provide," she continued. "What if He's providing us with Georg?"

Mammi whipped her head around to face her eldest child. "He did not—"

"But how do you know?" Elisabeth interrupted. "You say we shouldn't question God, so we will never know what His true intent is, but what if Georg is it?"

Mammi bent forward and threw her hair into the washing bowl. Elisabeth took the jug of water and poured it over Mammi's hair.

"You don't have to forgive him. But we know Peter-Bátschi can't help us—he has to look after his family and Omama—and your brothers-in-law also have their land, which is more than ours, and only their children and perhaps one or two day labourers to help. Konrad-Bátschi's family has the means to help us, and Georg and Samuel are offering."

"But is Konrad?" Mammi asked. "Georg would not answer that question. I will not get into more fights with your father's brother." She collected her hair together and squeezed the water out of it and into the bowl. Elisabeth passed her a cloth to dry her hair. "It's time for bed," Mammi said and opened the door to the front room. Elisabeth's siblings looked hopefully at her, but all she could do was shrug. She sent Rosina and Anna out to the kitchen to wash up and get changed.

Elisabeth looked up at Jesus. *If we can find that magazine and make those shoes, and if Mammi accepts Georg's help, then we might actually make it through this year without Tata. But I need You to help me with this.*

CHAPTER ELEVEN

*I*t was Sunday afternoon, and Opa sat out on the porch despite the frigid cold. He was sipping on a cup of chamomile tea, the German hour blaring on the radio in the kitchen so he could hear it outside.

Mom put on her coat. "The two of you are up to something," she said to Juliana and Sophie. "Usually Juliana's hunched over her books, studying, or in the basement practising. But you've been over a lot, Sophie." Mom's tone was curious but gentle.

Dad came into the kitchen to start packing food for his trip tomorrow.

"You must know what's going on," Mom said to him.

"What do you mean?"

Mom pointed to the two girls. "They're up to something. Juliana rarely has people over this often."

"Our daughter is finally getting to know the family and you're complaining?"

"Ha!" Mom said, a skeptical look on her face. "No offence, Sophie, but Juliana's never been a family person."

"In Juliana's defence," Dad said, "she didn't have family in Calgary."

Mom's eyes narrowed playfully to slits. "That's such a convenient excuse, Paul. You're in on this, too, aren't you?" Then her eyes lit up. "Is it for my birthday? You're doing something for my birthday, aren't you?" Juliana hadn't seen Mom this excited at home since...she couldn't remember when. "A party or something? A gift?"

Should Juliana tell her what was going on? Mom looked so happy. What was a few more days?

Dad kept their cover and shook his head. "I told you, my boss gave me short-haul trips this week so I can take you out on your birthday for dinner to that steakhouse you love so much down by that mall, and then on Saturday, Annie's cooking for everyone before Peter flies out. Now that Juliana's found someone who likes preparing lettuce, I think we should consider it a win-win for all of us."

Juliana and Sophie giggled. Sophie had told her once that she actually enjoyed ripping lettuce, because it let her help in the kitchen without worrying about cutting herself.

Mom sighed. "I guess I'm not going to get it out of you.

Oh, well." She buttoned her coat closed. "I'm heading to the pharmacy to fill Tata's prescription, and then to the bank. What are the two of you going to do now?"

Juliana had to think fast. "I thought I'd finally show Sophie some of my tap," she said and began heading to the basement. "You know, now that there won't be any power outages?"

"Where are your tap shoes, then?" Mom asked.

Juliana's cheeks burned. She ran to her room to get her shoes. "Let's go!" she said to Sophie and grabbed her by the arm before Mom could say anything more.

In the rec room, Juliana started pulling out her tap board from under the couch, but once she heard Mom leave through the side door, she let out a sigh of relief and pushed it back.

"You're horrible at lying," Sophie said, smiling.

"Really? You're the one who brought up the dance thing before."

"Okay, fine. We're both horrible at it."

"Agreed!"

"So," Sophie said with trepidation. "Are you ready?"

"Should we have a barf bucket in there?"

"Bathroom's close enough."

"I guess this is it then."

"I guess it is."

They had decided that vacuuming the dungeon would get rid of most of the bugs. In the laundry room, Juliana grabbed the vacuum cleaner—a heavy, grey one with a stiff hose and a horizontal canister whose wheels squeaked as it rolled—and handed Sophie a handheld vacuum. A minute later, they stood outside the dungeon.

Juliana plugged in the vacuum, opened the door, and without turning on the light, started vacuuming. Something clicked its way through the hose.

"Oh my god," Sophie said over the motor of the vacuum, "was that a bug?"

"How am I supposed to know? The light's off and I'm not looking!"

Juliana and Sophie broke into laughter as Juliana vacuumed a safe spot on the floor. When they were done, Juliana finally pulled the chain on the lightbulb.

"You know what? The entrance here already looks a bit better." She scanned the small cellar. "What do you want to do? Vacuum the jars? Or use the brush attachment to do the books?"

Sophie's shoulders drooped as she scanned the cement-enclosed room. "I guess give me something that..." Her face flushed. What was she worried about?

"I know it's gross, but I at least got everything off the floor at the doorway," Juliana said.

Sophie shook her head. "It's not that. It's nothing. I don't know—are there any empty shelves or something?" Sophie stared at the floor. "I just don't want to break anything. It's all really special to Opa or he wouldn't keep any of this."

The glasses, Rebecca's "training," the whispers…was this what'd been bothering Sophie? "Are you okay? Is there, I don't know, is there something you want to talk about?"

Juliana's cheeks burned as Sophie explained she'd sometimes knocked things over or dropped them because she hadn't seen everything someone had placed in her hands. Juliana felt embarrassed for her.

"Listen, why don't I just do it?" Juliana offered. "Besides, you're my sidekick, right? My cheerleader."

Sophie's face brightened up.

"But you have to cheer me on," Juliana said, hoping that would distract her cousin from her thoughts.

"That's right! Go team!" Sophie punched a fist in the air.

Juliana turned the vacuum back on and ran the brush attachment over some of the items. She handed things to Sophie to hold so Juliana could get into corners and tight spots, but she told Sophie exactly what she was placing in her hands each time. After about twenty minutes, Juliana announced that everything was as clean as she could get it without emptying the small room. The girls returned both vacuums to the laundry room and then stood outside the cellar.

"It doesn't look so hazy anymore," Juliana said.

"Even the air smells cleaner now," Sophie said. "We might have to stop calling it the dungeon." She stepped onto the cold cement floor and looked around. She slowly reached for a jar on the shelf but then pulled her hand back. Juliana took a jar down and placed it in Sophie's hands.

"It's just the jar, no lid or anything," she said.

Sophie turned the jar around in her hands. "So our grandmother would've used these?"

"I guess so."

"Mom said Oma made this really delicious plum jam of some kind. It had a funny name—Opa might remember it —but she said she's never had anything that tastes like it again."

Juliana felt a ping of jealousy. *Mom's never mentioned anything like that*, she thought. In fact, Juliana knew so little about this family. Just like Dad, Mom seemed to want to ignore her past. What was so horrible about it?

"That must have been some amazing jam," Juliana said. "But check out these books." She pulled one out of a box, and unlike at Christmas when she had first discovered the books, now no dehydrated bug carcasses fell off. Instead, the spines showed off their deep, navy blue colour. "It's heavy, though." She handed the encyclopedia to Sophie. "I think they're over a hundred years old."

"Whoa..." Sophie let her hand glide over the leather cover and spine. She opened it slowly. "Oh my god, it reeks!" She sneezed so hard that her hands flipped the book into the air, and it crashed, open side down, on the cement floor. Juliana gasped: the spines on these books creaked when they were opened. She hoped the fall hadn't actually broken it.

"I'm sorry," Sophie said, wrapping her arms around herself. "I really didn't mean it."

The middle of the spine creased inwards now, and pages were folded underneath themselves. Juliana knew those pages would never lie flat again. But judging by the expression on her cousin's face, she chose not to mention it. Sophie needed a friend now, just like Juliana had needed one when Rachel's mom had passed away and Sophie had been there for her.

"Well, I don't think anyone's read these for a long time," Juliana said. "I'm sure no one will notice." She straightened out the pages one by one when one slipped out. "Oh, crap."

Sophie hugged herself tighter, her eyes grew wet, and she bit her lip. "Did one rip out?"

"I think—" Juliana picked it up. "Wait a minute." She turned the piece of paper over in her hand. "No, there's handwriting on this. I think it's a letter. I can't read it but I'm sure it's a letter. You found a letter!"

Sophie wiped her eyes and smiled. "Really?"

"What are you girls doing down here?"

Both girls shrieked as they jumped.

"How did you—?" Sophie started.

"Where did—?" Juliana said at the same time.

Uncle Peter laughed. "Didn't mean to scare you. I

thought Brian and I would come over and listen to the German hour with Tata for a bit. I mean, to be honest, Brian can't stand that music, but what can I say? It's good memories for me. It's freezing out there so I came down to grab another blanket."

"We're still looking for that photo," Sophie said. "We're hoping it's in here somewhere."

Uncle Peter whistled. "You girls must be desperate. I haven't seen this cellar look this clean in, like, forever. What do you have in your hand there, Juliana?"

Juliana handed their uncle the letter.

As his eyes traveled over the document, Juliana wondered if he was actually reading it. She had her answer moments later. "It's a letter from Omama to her father."

Juliana's eyes popped out. "You read German, too?"

Uncle Peter laughed. "That's usually what happens when you speak a language." How could one person be this happy all the time? He was weirding Juliana out. "Tata taught me quite a bit when I worked in the factory when I wasn't much older than the two of you. Then I took a few more courses at university, went on exchange, and *voilà*! It's a useful language for an industrial engineer. I speak French, too, and Brian's teaching me some Japanese. He still speaks it with his grandparents."

"Oh," Juliana said.

"I know. TMI from an old guy."

No, just a weird guy, Juliana thought. *But weird in a good way.*

"What does it say?" Sophie asked, bringing the subject back to the letter.

Uncle Peter translated it into English as he read it aloud.

March 12, 1920

Dear Tata,

Thank you for your postcard. It was a wonderful surprise! We were all very happy to hear from you.

I wish I could write you and say that I am doing well, but I am not. I have been studying hard for my confirmation, but there are some things I cannot figure out. They have to do with your family.

You know that Georg succumbs to these horrific fits. I've seen them now, and I'm greatly troubled. Before you left, you told me to be strong and do what Jesus would want me to do. But I don't know what that is.

God wants me to obey my parents and to help and forgive our fellow man. Mammi forbids me from helping Georg, but when I help him, I feel warm inside. I believe I'm doing God's will. What tormented soul does not benefit from friendship?

But I now know about Georg's promise to protect Andreas-Bátschi. That must make Mammi very angry, and I understand why she dislikes your family so much.

But he and Samuel and a friend, Stefan Schäfer, have helped us several times now. I know Mammi has a brother and several brothers-in-law, but Peter-Bátschi takes to the bottle now and can be

"That's where it stops," Uncle Peter said.

"Georg!" Juliana exclaimed, and Uncle Peter and Sophie looked at her, confused. "You don't understand. Opa says Georg wasn't a man. He said he wouldn't help his family. But—read it again!"

Surprised by her reaction, Uncle Peter re-read the letter.

"'Horrific fits,'" Juliana quoted. "That has to be PTSD. Can you read it again?"

"What on earth are you talking about?" Sophie asked. "You're making no sense whatsoever. How can a man not be a man? Maybe he didn't self-identify as a man or something?"

Uncle Peter smiled. "The world has changed a lot since then. No, Sophie, that's not it. Opa is a man of his generation, so he holds a few...beliefs...that aren't really kosher today."

"I still don't get it," Sophie said. Juliana didn't either, but their uncle answered before she could say anything.

"Don't worry about it. He loves you and that's all you need to care about." He pulled out his phone and took a picture of the letter. "Why don't I type this up at home and email it to you?"

Juliana jumped up and down again. "Could you? Please? Do you want it, too, Sophie?"

Sophie still looked confused. "Um, I guess so, but I have no idea who...what's his name?"

"Georg. Like from *The Sound of Music*. Georg von Trapp?"

Sophie shrugged her shoulders.

"Your mom never showed you any musicals?"

Sophie shook her head.

Uncle Peter passed Juliana his phone to type in her email address and Juliana handed him the encyclopedia to hold.

"Is this where you found it?" he asked, and she nodded. "'*Galizien*,'" he read and then explained, "Galicia. Not in Spain, in Eastern Europe." He read to himself first, mumbling a little as he went.

"You can read that, too?" Juliana asked in amazement.

"Slowly." He turned to Sophie. "It's in a script we often call Gothic. It's very decorative. Modr's old Bible was written in it. She forced me to read some of it for...well, let's just say she was hoping I'd change." Uncle Peter placed the letter back in its spot and closed the book. "Seems like the proper place to store it. I wonder if this Georg fought here. I don't know much about the Eastern front in World War One, but Galicia was a major part of it. Maybe that's why the letter's in here." He smiled again. "I'd better get back upstairs before Brian goes mad with the music and Opa goes mad with Brian." He handed the book back to Juliana and she gave him his phone.

"Do you think the photo's here?" Juliana asked, indicating the dungeon.

Uncle Peter looked around and shook his head. "If your mom didn't destroy it, and it's not in the living room, then Modr must have sent it to family in Europe. They were always mailing photos back and forth. Sorry—I wish I had a better idea for you." He returned upstairs.

Dejected, Juliana and Sophie collapsed on the couch in the rec room.

"Europe?" Sophie asked.

"I guess that's that."

"Well, at least the dungeon's clean."

They sat in silence for a few minutes. The girls really needed a break now, especially after all the frustrations in searching for this photo.

"Café in Belmont Village?" she offered Sophie.

"Totally."

CHAPTER TWELVE

Georg sat silently atop the horse that pulled the wagon over the gravel road. Elisabeth, Rosina, and Stefan sat in the wagon, bumping and jiggling about as the wooden wheels rolled over different stones and grooves. Baskets of corn kernels rattled, as though they were trying to pop out of their containers and avoid the inevitable: planting. The group had already left the village and were now traveling up the road to the family's *salasch*.

Elisabeth shook her head. "I don't know what to do anymore. I think this idea of making a new kind of shoe would be good for us, but Mammi won't change. Why does she have to be so stubborn?"

Stefan looked out over the flat valleys of farmland that

stretched for kilometres on either side of the road. "People like your mother are still holding on to memories," he said. "If things don't change, then it's comfortable. I can understand that. For the years I was gone, nothing kept me alive more than the thought of returning home and finding everything just as it was. I wanted to forget the war, to live the rest of my life as though it never happened."

The wagon travelled along, the crackling gravel and shaking kernels filling Elisabeth's ears. She looked up at Georg. Everything had changed for him and had changed *him*. Because he had fought, he now relived the nightmares of war and his deceased family day and night.

But was all change bad? The fashions in Maria's magazine looked exciting and fresh! Elisabeth reached up to touch her headscarf, which she wore today to protect herself from the elements, and wondered what beautiful things she could do with her hair instead of always tying it up in the same braids. If she cut it short, for example, she wouldn't have to spend so much time brushing it. Or maybe she could keep it long but braid it in a different way. *But when would I have the time to learn how?*

Stefan sighed. "Unfortunately, the war has shown us that the world is changing, and Semlak is part of that world. Some of that change has been good, of course. I think it would be a good idea if Frau Schuhmacher made fancier shoes." Elisabeth was delighted that Stefan thought the same way she did. "Do you know where the magazine is, Rosina?" he asked.

Elisabeth couldn't tell if Rosina had heard the question because her youngest sister was staring at Stefan's missing arm.

"Rosina?" Elisabeth asked. "Stefan asked you a question."

Rosina shook her head.

"I'm sorry," Elisabeth said to Stefan, but Stefan smiled back at her. *How can he be so happy all the time?* Elisabeth thought. *Especially after being in Siberia for two years?*

He inched toward Rosina a little and reached out his stump. The sleeve on his coat, like his other clothing, had been hemmed short, presumably by Stefan's mother. Elisabeth couldn't imagine how she would feel if she had to shorten all of Luki's sleeves.

"Would you like to touch my arm?" Stefan asked Rosina.

Rosina's eyes opened wide and she rapidly shook her head. "Then I'll lose my arm, too!"

Elisabeth covered her face with her hands but Stefan broke out in laughter, surprising Elisabeth.

"Nothing will happen to you," Stefan said. "I promise."

Rosina glanced at Elisabeth, who nodded. Stefan reached the stump of his arm out.

"Does it hurt?" Rosina asked.

"Not anymore."

Not anymore, Elisabeth thought. How long had it taken before his arm had stopped hurting? How much had it hurt when he lost it? Elisabeth pushed the disturbing thoughts out of her mind.

Rosina swallowed. In a flash, she held out her doll to touch Stefan's amputated arm and then jerked it back to her chest. Elisabeth had to giggle: sometimes her sister's youthful fears were indeed funny. Stefan and Rosina shared a smile. Rosina then reached out with her own hand and touched Stefan's sleeve with her finger. She drew a line around the end of his upper arm and up to his shoulder. Without saying another word, she hugged her doll again and smiled at Stefan.

Elisabeth smiled at him, too. Despite everything he had endured during the war and at the POW camp, he was still a kind man.

THE WAGON TURNED LEFT DOWN ANOTHER GRAVEL ROAD AT the corner of the family's *salasch*. Konrad-Bátschi's family owned the house and everything belonging to it, including the equipment shed, animal stalls, the barn, and all the land up to the corner where they had just turned. Now they had reached the small parcel of land that belonged to Elisabeth's family.

As the wagon pulled up to the house, Elisabeth saw Deaf Lissi whitewashing the walls outside, something Elisabeth and Mammi had done to their home a week before. It was the custom every spring, before Easter, that the women give all walls in the homes—inside and out—a fresh coat of lime wash.

Georg pulled on the reins, stopping the horse, as Samuel limped out to greet them, several thick, wooden sticks in his hand. He set the sticks down by the cart and he and Stefan helped the two girls out of the wagon. The wind outside the village blew harshly over the flat fields despite the warming spring air. Elisabeth retied her shawl, crossing it over her chest and knotting the ends behind her back as usual. She then did the same for Rosina.

"Lissi has more shawls if you need them," Samuel offered, and Elisabeth thanked him but declined for now—she had brought more herself. Besides, she would warm up once she started planting.

Georg remained with the horse and lit a cigarette. Deaf Lissi stopped painting, wiped her hands on a rag, and came over to greet them.

"Welcome, Lissika," she said to Elisabeth as they clasped hands and kissed each other on the cheeks. Deaf Lissi's grip was strong, befitting her stocky, large-boned stature.

Deaf Lissi said hello to Rosina and Stefan and merely

acknowledged Georg's presence with a nod to her brother-in-law.

"I'm going to help them plant seed," Samuel said to his wife, and Elisabeth caught a look of displeasure on her face. Elisabeth couldn't blame her, though. Samuel also saw the look and added, "Just until we get things sorted out with Lissa-Néni."

His comment caught Elisabeth's ear. It meant Samuel and Georg hadn't given up yet on Mammi! If this exchange was still a possibility, Elisabeth had to show her family's willingness to help Georg's family.

"We will definitely repay you," Elisabeth offered. "I could take home some of your sewing or help you with canning once the fruit has ripened. My sisters are old enough to help with those chores, too."

Deaf Lissi's face relaxed at Elisabeth's offer and she thanked her before returning to her whitewashing.

Samuel handed one stick to Stefan, another to Elisabeth, and he kept the third one for himself. Georg retrieved some sacks from the wagon, and the men each put one around their neck and filled it with corn. Stefan beckoned to Rosina to join him, and she ran to keep up, which relieved Elisabeth. It meant she could talk more with Georg.

The moist spring earth sucked at their feet as they trudged out to the far edge of the empty field, near the wheat. The farther portion of Tata's fields—about three-quarters—was filled with winter wheat, while the closer portion—the one already ploughed—would be used for corn, with one row left for broom corn.

Samuel took the first row by himself, Stefan and Rosina the next two, and Elisabeth and Georg the fourth and fifth rows.

"You follow Stefan's directions, Rosina, understood?"

Rosina nodded. Stefan asked her to hold out her hands, placed a small handful of corn in them, and explained what she had to do. He took his stick, jabbed it into the ground several centimetres—one hole in each row—and then asked Rosina to place several kernels in each hole and cover them up while he made the next two.

"She's lucky," Elisabeth said to Georg. "She's short—the ground is closer to her hands." Elisabeth's attempt at a joke elicited nothing from Georg and a scowl from Rosina.

The earth swallowed up the kernels one by one as Elisabeth and Georg slowly worked their way down their rows, with Elisabeth making the holes and Georg throwing a few kernels in and then covering them. When they stopped to look back, they could only see their footprints as proof that they had planted.

"Thank you for your offer," Elisabeth began. "Mammi still hasn't accepted. We want her to, all of us do, but she won't."

"I understand."

"But I spoke with her about it again last night, and she seemed to at least be thinking about it."

Georg said nothing and the two cousins continued down their rows, pressing kernels into the ground and covering them. After a few more metres, Elisabeth had to stand and stretch: her knees weren't used to the bending. She looked behind her and then ahead of her. *Jesus, help me to survive today*, she prayed. She took a few steps forward, crouched, grabbed a few kernels out of the pail with each hand, and shoved them into the ground on either side of her.

"Your family can't do this alone," Georg said.

"I know. Trust me, I know! But Mammi's concerned about..." She felt rude complaining about Georg's father to his face.

"It's none of his concern," Georg replied. He obviously knew what Elisabeth was going to say. "He pretends that this land is still his, but when Samuel moved into the *salasch*, Tata gave it to him. The workshop, vineyard, and house in the village will become mine when Tata dies. They have nothing to do with your family."

When Tata dies. Georg's expressionless face made those words sound even colder than they were.

"Mammi doesn't want more fights with him," Elisabeth explained. "That's what she said." Most conversations with Margarethe-Néni and Konrad-Bátschi involved underhanded comments and insults hidden inside compliments. "I want to talk to her again and see if I can still change her mind. We're not going make it through this season without your help."

Georg nodded and the two continued in silence when suddenly Rosina let out a scream. Georg bound over the rows of the field to help. Elisabeth ran, too, arriving a few seconds afterwards. Samuel also rushed over.

"I'm so sorry," Stefan said as he tried to comfort Rosina. Elisabeth could tell he was also trying to shield her hand from Georg's eyes. "I didn't see this bit of cornstalk still in the ground. She cut herself on it."

Crying, Rosina stared at her hand and pushed it out toward Elisabeth, as though expecting her to fix it. Blood dripped from a gash that crossed the bottom of her palm.

Georg took a few steps back, and Elisabeth looked up at him. His breathing quickened and his eyes opened wide.

"Georg, listen to me," Stefan said. He jumped to his feet and stood between Georg and Rosina. "I'm here with you."

Samuel placed a hand on his brother's shoulder. He, too, spoke to Georg but in a low voice. Elisabeth couldn't hear what he said. Assuming Rosina's cut had awakened a bad memory in their cousin, she yanked her young sister up, startling her and causing her to cry in protest. But Elisabeth knew she had to get Rosina out of there. She led Rosina through the mud as fast as she could, Elisabeth constantly glancing over her shoulder, thankful not only that Stefan and Samuel were there to help but that Rosina was too focused on her hand to watch Georg. They reached the house in no time.

Deaf Lissi cleaned off her hands to help. "There he goes again," she mumbled under her breath, looking back at Georg. Then her demeanour changed as she knelt down to Rosina's level. "Let's see. Oh, that's nothing, Rosi."

"It hurts!" Rosina wailed.

Deaf Lissi offered to take Rosina inside to clean it up and Rosina nodded. Deaf Lissi leaned over to Elisabeth, "I'll look after her hand, and then she doesn't have to see that man become possessed by the devil." Before Elisabeth could say anything further, Deaf Lissi led Rosina, still crying but calmer now, into the house. How many people would Elisabeth have to explain this to? Georg couldn't prevent these nightmares.

Yet, why couldn't she hear Georg's shouts? She turned around to see what was happening. To her surprise, Georg, Samuel, and Stefan were still standing and talking. Had his spell not begun yet? Curious, but also wanting to help, she trudged back through the mud to the men. Samuel pulled out a packet of cigarettes from Georg's vest pocket, opened it so Georg could pull one out, put it back, and then struck a match for him. Georg breathed in deeply to light the cigarette. By the time Elisabeth had reached them, Georg appeared calm again.

Had Jesus healed him? It was Lent. Was this perhaps one of Jesus's miracles?

"WAIT HERE," ELISABETH SAID TO ROSINA THE NEXT morning. It was time to leave to get the mail and hear the week's news. Elisabeth was certain she'd run into Georg and Stefan, so she told Rosina she thought she'd ask Mammi one more time about Georg's offer.

Surprisingly, Rosina looked up from her knitting. "Do you think she'll say yes?"

Elisabeth shrugged. "I hope so. Say a little prayer to Jesus for me."

Rosina dropped her knitting on the table and immediately folded her hands together and looked up at the crucifix that hung above the doorway. Her lips moved as she mumbled something.

As Elisabeth walked along the house under the overhang to the workshop, she repeated in her mind the tasks she needed help with: building a stove for the workshop, caring for their fields, finding the magazine, and if the discussion went well, making different shoes. Georg and Stefan had previously offered to help with the stove, both men and Samuel with the fields, Anna and Rosina with the shoes, *and*, Elisabeth sighed, *no one to help me find Maria's magazine.*

She took a deep breath and pushed open the door, the stench of feet and leather greeting her. Elisabeth wrinkled her nose: she couldn't imagine working in this dingy, stinky workshop day in and day out. A small stove would produce more heat and allow Mammi to open the door more, especially now that spring had arrived.

"I know why you're here," Mammi said, her voice firm. She hammered a nail into the heel of a man's boot.

"Mammi—"

"Do not interrupt me."

Elisabeth swallowed and prayed to Jesus for help.

Mammi picked up another nail, held it in place, and hammered it in.

"I do not like how often you question me," she said. "I am your mother, and you are to listen to me."

"I'm—"

Mammi shushed her daughter and continued. "It has been four months now since Tata left us, and it has been hard on all of us, including me." Mammi placed the hammer on the table and finally looked up. "But a mother knows when her child is growing up. Jesus showed me last night when you spoke to me in private." She stood up and massaged her lower back. "I cannot forgive Georg. He promised to protect my brother, and yet that ogre of a man survived and my brother died."

Elisabeth remained silent. She couldn't guess what Mammi was going to say. On one hand, Mammi had paid her a rare compliment. On the other, it sounded like she wasn't going to accept Georg's offer. Elisabeth became impatient: she didn't want to miss the postman and the week's news, but Mammi still hadn't finished speaking.

"Stefan may build a small stove in here," Mammi said. "Not Georg. I do not want to see him. If it takes Stefan longer because he has one arm, so be it. You will cook for him when he is here and send food home with him for his family. That is our payment. I'm certain someone has leftover bricks we can use. You will have to ask around. And let Stefan arrange with a Gypsy to finish the stove."

Elisabeth's heart almost leaped into her throat with joy. This decision meant the workshop would become more comfortable for Mammi, and things would be easier for her baby. Assuming that was all she needed to hear, Elisabeth took a step toward the door.

"Lissika, I am not done!"

Elisabeth froze and turned back to face Mammi.

"I have not decided about Georg's offer yet. But this baby is coming. My sisters may help me raise it, but I haven't told them yet. Either way..." She didn't finish her sentence. "I know you are going out to the postman today, and that Georg will likely be there. Tell him to come see me today, after two o'clock." She sat back down and resumed her work. "I will decide by then."

Elisabeth's face broke into a huge grin. Mammi was

willing to speak with Georg! It meant she might change her mind! "Thank you, Mammi! Thank you!"

Mammi's lips remained tight and straight. "Stop that. You look like a stupid donkey."

But Elisabeth didn't care. She ran out of the workshop to tell Rosina that Jesus had answered her prayers, and to head into town with the good news.

CHAPTER THIRTEEN

"Oh my god."

Re-energized from a snack at the café, Juliana and Sophie tried to make one last attempt at finding the photo. The surprise party was this coming Saturday, and Juliana couldn't let the idea of a perfect birthday gift go. Aside from Mom's happy moment when she had explained Opa's reorganized closet to him, she seemed constantly worried about work and about Opa. Juliana had completed the bare minimum of her homework for the weekend so she had time to try once more.

To cover their intent, Juliana and Sophie offered to shovel Opa's driveway so they'd have an excuse to look in the garage for five minutes while they got out shovels.

The detached, single-car garage had piles of boxes

stacked upon boxes stacked upon boxes...it was never ending.

"This looks worse than the dungeon," Juliana said.

"But not as smelly," Sophie added. "I'm ready!"

Sophie stepped closer to the boxes and walked along them to the space between the wall of cardboard and Opa's workbench. She reached her arm through, then her shoulder, sucked in her stomach until it was concave, and then pushed her body through with a grunt. Juliana tried to follow her just in case she did fit, but she couldn't. She peeked into the space instead.

"Sophie, be careful. There are several tool boxes there, and a few of them have rusty tools hanging out."

"Got it." Sophie carefully scanned the workbench. "I don't see anywhere here, anyways, where Opa could keep photos."

"What do you see behind the boxes?"

Sophie turned around and peered into the back of the garage. "Before you moved here...yup. It's all still here, I think. It's really dark, but it looks like Opa's old lawnmower, trimmer, a bunch of gardening tools...Maybe I'm missing something, but I don't think anything here has moved in the last few years."

Sophie squeezed her way back out from behind the boxes. "Talk about a waste of time." She lifted a shovel off a rack that hung by the entrance door to the garage. "I guess we're shovelling for nothing," she said.

"Sorry," Juliana replied and grabbed her own shovel. "I guess that's it."

They stepped outside with their shovels.

"I'm sorry again," Juliana said. "But thanks for trying to help me."

"Yeah, no worries. I have to admit, it was kind of fun. Though failing at this sucks."

"Tell me about it. It's almost as bad as my marks from last semester."

The cousins shovelled Opa's driveway for about ten minutes. The sinking feeling in Juliana grew as the mounds of snow climbed. She had been so sure the photo existed, and Mom really needed something uplifting now. Juliana knew Mom liked the closet idea, but it didn't make her happy enough. What else could she give Mom that would really lift up her spirits? A necklace? Of what? Mom rarely wore jewellery as it was—she didn't want to lose it at work. Same with makeup. Mom had told Juliana once that she had to demonstrate how to cut onions when she'd first started with the chain. The mascara gave her Alice Cooper eyes by the time she'd finished the demonstration. "That was the last time I ever wore makeup to work," she'd said. Mom liked to read, but the only downside to where they lived was the lack of a nearby bookstore, and Juliana wasn't going to pay for express shipping.

"Hey, girls!" Aunt Anne called. Juliana hadn't heard her or the rest of the family approach: she'd been too absorbed in her own disappointment and shovelling. Aunt Anne was carrying a covered casserole dish, Rebecca a large salad bowl, and Uncle Phillip a dish stacked high with brownies. Sophie's other siblings trailed behind, the whole clan looking like a mini-parade.

"Where are your sunglasses, Sophie?" Aunt Anne asked.

Sophie looked at the ground. "In the house."

"You know what the doctor said."

"Yeah."

Aunt Anne looked at Juliana and then again at her daughter. "I'm not going to ruin tonight with another lecture." She flashed Rebecca a stern look. "And neither will you." She adjusted her mood again instantly. "Tata said he wanted to host all of us here, so I offered to cook."

"Good idea," Juliana said as her stomach growled. "If you'd asked Mom to cook this much, we'd all be waiting until tomorrow!"

Everyone laughed at the joke as they entered the house.

"But if I'm not mistaken," replied Sophie as she and Juliana returned their shovels, "you're not super-fast either."

Juliana playfully punched Sophie in the arm. "I've still got thirty years to learn."

THE SCHUHMACHERS, ROTHS, MORGANS AND BRIAN HAD squeezed into the kitchen, leaving barely any room to walk. Aunt Anne had made little Scott go to the washroom before sitting down because he had had to sit in the very middle at the back of the table, bookended by his siblings: Charlie and Dean on one side and Rebecca and Tony on the other. Dad and Brian had carried up a small table and more chairs from the basement, extending the dinner table into the tiny cooking area, and everyone sat shoulder to shoulder. Juliana couldn't wait for everyone to get up—the closeness felt like being in a tiny room with little space to dance—but everyone was laughing at something Uncle Peter was saying.

"Oh yeah," Uncle Peter said. "Those old German women are still the same. You could stand in one spot, they'd walk into you, and then they'd yell at you for being in their way."

Everyone at the table found the observation funny, except Opa.

"It's because you should step out of their way when they're coming toward you. It's called respect, something young folks don't have these days."

Uncle Peter, Aunt Anne, and Mom all rolled their eyes.

"Tata," Aunt Anne said, "they even do that when you're in a crowd and have nowhere to go. Or has that changed, Peter?"

"Nope, right, Brian?"

"Yup."

Dad patted his stomach. "Well, thank you Anne for such a wonderful meal."

"My pleasure," Aunt Anne replied. "It's nice to have our baby brother home for a little."

With supper finally over, Juliana and Sophie could go hang out in the basement. They'd given up on their search for the photo; they just wanted to see what else was in the dungeon, now that it was clean. Maybe another book of drawings?

Aunt Anne and Mom stood up, and Aunt Anne reached for Katy's plate.

"Still taking Katy's stuff?" Uncle Peter said, his usual huge smile on his face.

"I'd take yours," Aunt Anne said, "but boys have cooties."

"Don't start that again," Opa said. "Aren't you three old enough to get along?"

"You know," Mom said to Aunt Anne, "I've been so busy these past two weeks, I forgot to ask you about an old photo I was wondering about." She placed a pile of dishes in the sink and Aunt Anne and Juliana exchanged glances. "I don't know if you remember it. It's me in a fuzzy white costume. I remember you and me arguing about it—I thought I looked like a complete idiot and you said I was lucky."

Aunt Anne carried over another pile of dishes while

Dad and Uncle Phillip moved chairs into the living room so Mom could open the dishwasher.

"I think I remember it," Aunt Anne said.

Mom pulled the dishwasher door down. "I was bawling my eyes out for an hour in our room, and you were shouting at me about how stupid I was for not seeing how special the whole thing was." Mom faced Aunt Anne. "I ran into Tanya at Juliana's competition. Remember her?"

Aunt Anne nodded.

"Ah, that photo!" Opa said and Juliana shot him a look that said he should stop talking. To her surprise, he understood. "I was just thinking about it," he said. "You said yesterday how wonderful Yulika looked in her dance costumes, and that one was your jazz solo. The first jazz solo you did in competition. You were adorable, Katy."

Opa did remember! That meant the picture had to be somewhere. Juliana's mind started to race.

"Do you know what happened to it?" Mom asked Opa.

Juliana held her breath. His memory seemed to be working right now!

CHAPTER FOURTEEN

"Jesus must be smiling on me today!" Elisabeth exclaimed as she jumped up and down, holding a letter from Tata in her hand. Stefan looked like he was ready to hug her. To her disappointment, though, Georg hadn't come to see the postman. Stefan said that Georg had needed to help his father because the parts for the Haibach order had come in.

"Let me hold the letter!" Rosina cried out, reaching up with her bandaged hand.

"No," Elisabeth said. "You're going to rip it."

Rosina's mouth turned upside down and Elisabeth threatened her with more housework if she said another word of complaint.

"Aren't you going to open it?" Stefan asked.

Elisabeth tucked the letter in to her purse. "Not out here. I'd like to read it in private." She closed her purse. "But I have some good news."

"Oh?"

"Mammi has accepted your offer to build her a small stove." Then she remembered Mammi's one condition and her smile drooped. "But Georg can't help."

Stefan's exuberance disappeared, too. "She can't forgive him, can she?"

Elisabeth shook her head. "However, she did ask me to have him come to our house sometime after two today. She wants to talk to him more about looking after our land."

Stefan scratched the back of his neck. "Did we win the war?"

Elisabeth laughed. "I think she now realizes how hard this season will be, and that Georg and Samuel are the only ones who can really help us right now."

"I can, too," Stefan added.

Elisabeth blushed.

"Are we going?" Rosina asked.

Elisabeth nodded. They started walking in the direction of the Schuhmacher home.

"I'm heading over to Georg's now," Stefan said. "He wanted me to bring the week's news."

"Do you mind passing along Mammi's message?"

"Why don't you give him the good news yourself?"

"I would if he were here, but going to my uncle's house...?" She could no longer look her aunt and uncle in the eyes after she had witnessed how terribly they treated their son. Just thinking about it sickened her.

"I see," Stefan said. "I can tell him. After Galicia and Siberia, no one scares me anymore."

"Galicia is where you fought?"

"Both of us. Actually, all of us. The entire thirty-third regiment."

Elisabeth wanted to ask more about his experiences—Stefan seemed comfortable talking about them—but the few details she knew had brought her to tears. She chose to change the subject to a topic she hoped wouldn't involve stories about body parts.

"Yesterday," Elisabeth said, "I was certain Georg was going to have another fit, but you and Samuel somehow calmed him down. What did you say this time?" Stefan had explained to her before that sometimes telling Georg the war was finished and that he could go home helped his fits end faster, though it could never prevent them. Had he found a way to prevent them now?

Stefan gave an uneasy glance toward Rosina, and Elisabeth guessed that what he wanted to say wasn't fit for young ears. She sent her sister off to the Bartolfs to play.

"There was a man in the camp—Heinrich," Stefan said. "From Berlin. He joined the war at the very end. His father was a doctor who treated men who'd come back from war. Heinrich said that men who had nightmares and other symptoms suffered from something called 'shell shock.' Some men couldn't even stop shaking. He said his father had cured some men of it, but not most. We certainly didn't have any doctors in Siberia to help the men who were suffering. Like Georg, they were ridiculed by many in the camp, especially the guards. We had to learn to help the men ourselves, and something that sometimes worked was distracting them before their nightmares took hold."

"But you've been by his side before when they've happened. Why did it work this time?" Elisabeth hoped her question didn't make Stefan feel like she was accusing him of anything. She really did want to know what the difference was, if there was one.

Stefan stared at the ground as they walked and pressed his fist into the small of his back, as though it were waiting for his other hand to join it, the way men often clasped their hands behind their back. He remained silent for a moment, as though he was thinking about something. Elisabeth waited.

"I told you yesterday," Stefan said, "how I prayed that Semlak would be the same when I returned. It gave me strength to survive."

"Yes, I remember. Do you find everything is the same?"

Stefan nodded. "Germans live on the north side of the main street, everyone else on the south side, and the

Gypsies in their settlement outside the village. Church is Sundays. Everyone wears the same clothes every Sunday. Weddings are Tuesdays and Thursdays. No dances during Lent. Just like before I left for war. I can barely tell we've even changed countries. However, what I didn't expect was that I would change."

Elisabeth wondered what he meant. She hadn't known Stefan before his return last month; their congregation had just over one thousand people. However, given that she would have been only eleven when he left, and he would have looked like every other young man in their church—he had had both arms then—it was under-standable.

He continued. "When your life depends on someone else, you don't care what he eats, what language he speaks, or what god he worships. He saved your life, and you do the same for him. It's war. I've only been home maybe a month, and I find I no longer care if someone is Christian or Jewish, German or Gypsy. I don't care if they show up to church ten minutes late or if the women don't bake perfect cakes. But everyone else still does. When I hear what my mother gossips about with her friends...I shake my head. There's so much pain out there, Elisabeth, and they're complaining that a woman has a crease in the wrong spot on her skirt."

A few people passed by. Elisabeth waved to the women, and Stefan nodded to the men.

"Why do you wear what you do?" Stefan asked once the people had passed.

Elisabeth looked down at her dress. "Because it's what I'm supposed to wear."

"All right. But why?"

Elisabeth thought hard. It was what German women wore. What other reason was there? A dress was certainly not the most practical style of clothing, though it could be cool in the summer. Moreover, women's Sunday clothing required hours of washing and ironing. A small mistake, like a crease in the wrong place, and Elisabeth had to start from scratch.

"I don't know," she finally said. "I guess it's how we've always dressed, isn't it?"

"It's tradition," Stefan said. "Just like the houses are always white with blue gables, German girls wear skirts with aprons, blouses with specific decorations on them, and they have their hair up in the same braids almost all the time."

"We also all wear the same kinds of shoes," she added.

"Exactly. But there is no tradition for the fallout of war." Stefan pushed his hand into his pocket and glanced at Elisabeth. "Which means there is no tradition for helping a man with his nightmares. Everyone in the village will talk about Georg, spread rumours about him, belittle him, even beat him. It will follow him to his grave. And it's not just here: it was like this in the camp, and I saw it in villages and cities on the journey home." Stefan stopped for a moment again and faced Elisabeth. Was he about to cry? His eyes looked slightly red. This discussion was becoming too personal. "Elisabeth, I saw men like me begging on the streets. The war ended two years ago, and men who were missing an arm, a leg, or more were begging on the streets. That's how their countries and families treat them. Some men were shaking uncontrollably, others were shouting out, like Georg. Believe me—even though everyone here is cruel to him, there is much worse out there." He blinked a few times and continued walking. "Spending time on the *salasch* seems to relax Georg and he has fewer episodes when he's there. But he still has them. I was just lucky yesterday."

So God had not cured Georg. Worse yet, Georg would likely live with these nightmares for the rest of his life, like so many other former soldiers. The war replaying inside one's mind whenever it pleased. Was this what hell was like?

ELISABETH STOOD OUTSIDE MAMMI'S WORKSHOP, TATA'S letter in hand. She read it again.

My dear, dear family,

Thank you for your letters. I am well. Like you, we

had sickness in our neighbourhood, but God spared my life this time, and those of other Semlakers who live here.

My golden one, you asked so many questions, I do not know if I can answer them all. Keep praying to Jesus that He may help you find your answers. I know you have your confirmation on Palm Sunday. When I am at church, I will be thinking of you. Study hard and do not disappoint us. God is watching you, especially on this day.

I work indoors, and it is hard. The smell is very strong from cigars. But I am earning well and that is the reason why I am here. Harrisburg is a large city, like Arad or Temeswar, so there is much opportunity for me here.

Something else I enjoy about this city is that you hear the news every day. Sometimes it is from the newspaper —it comes out daily here, like it does in Arad—and sometimes it is on the radio—some of the Semlakers have one. I am not surprised that prisoners of war are still coming out of Russia. The situation there is very bad. I can only pray that ~~Hungary~~ Romania never falls to these Communists.

I miss all of you and am sorry that I am not there to help with the planting season and wheat harvest. Hopefully you are able to find help. If you cannot, speak to Konrad. I have written him, too, and asked that he help look after you.

Your,

Tata and Husband

Elisabeth had it in Tata's own handwriting: Tata wanted them to ask his family for help. She took a deep breath, pushed open the door, and walked in.

"Tata has written," she said to Mammi, and Mammi stopped working.

CHAPTER FIFTEEN

"No," Opa said. "That's my problem. I can't find it either."

Mom returned to loading the dishwasher. "That's too bad. Tanya made me realize that Anne was right back then, that it was a really special role. I was so angry and embarrassed when I actually had a special opportunity."

Uncle Peter was right. Mom did regret something. But that was so long ago...why did it matter now?

"Board game, anyone?" Uncle Peter asked.

Everyone declined, lamenting at how full they were from the delicious food.

"Rebecca, Tony, you two help with the dishes," Aunt Anne said. "Paul and Katy have to leave early in the morning to go to work. Put the leftover lasagna and salad in the fridge here for them."

Without a complaint, Sophie's two oldest siblings joined their mother at the sink. Opa, Dad, Uncle Peter, Uncle Phillip, and Brian stayed at the kitchen table and promised to carry the chairs and extra table down later. Mom helped with putting the dishes away.

That photo was somewhere. *Think!* Juliana told herself. "Let's go, before they figure out something for us to do," she whispered to Sophie. The two snuck down the stairs, though Juliana feared the creaking steps would give away their escape. Suddenly, an idea flew into Juliana's brain and she slapped her head. "Wait a minute! Board games!"

She rushed past Sophie, darted into the laundry room, and began shoving the boxes in front of the closet door to the side.

"Stop," she said to Sophie as she entered. "Turn to your right. Do you see that shelf up there?" Sophie nodded. "The flashlights are there. Just pull one down."

"I don't know..." Sophie said.

"You'll be fine," Juliana replied. "Besides, they look really cheap. If one breaks, I don't think anyone will care."

While Sophie retrieved a flashlight, Juliana began emptying the closet, making sure to push everything as far off to the side as possible but still warning Sophie about the mess.

"I can see those things," Sophie said. "They're huge. It's the small things in front of me that I can't see."

"Got it." Juliana guided Sophie to hold the flashlight so

it shone to the end of the closet, illuminating the foot of the stairs. She saw what she needed to see.

"Get Scott," she told Sophie. "He's small enough to fit in here and won't mind the bugs." She took the flashlight from Sophie, who returned upstairs to get her youngest brother, and pointed it to her target: an old, battered board game box with the word "Frustration" on the side.

"What do you want?" Scott said, his arms crossed when he came down.

"I need you to get something for me," Juliana said.

"No."

Sophie intervened. "Remember what I told you upstairs? It's like a superhero adventure. You get to crawl in like an insect and pull out a few things for us. It's dark and scary in there."

Good ploy, Juliana thought about Sophie's tactic. "And we need someone small enough to reach in," she added.

"Awesome!" Scott got down on this hands and knees and crawled in.

"Get that game of *Frustration*," Juliana said.

"How do you spell that?"

Juliana smiled. He was cute when he wasn't trying to shoot her in one of his imaginary adventure games. "It starts with an F. Get me the box that starts with an F."

Scott came back out with it in his hands.

"What else?" Scott asked, his eyes bright.

"That was it," Sophie said. "That was the mission! But now, you can't tell anyone about it, okay?"

Scott hesitated.

"Okay...?" Sophie tried one more time. "It's a surprise..."

Without answering, Scott ran back upstairs.

"I hope he doesn't say anything," Sophie said.

But Juliana brimmed with excitement. She didn't care. She pressed the box into Sophie's hands. "Open it! I'll bet the photo's in there."

Sophie lifted the lid, and there it was: a somewhat yellowed photo of Mom as a girl, wearing rainbow stockings and a white bag of fake fur from the top of her head to past her bottom. Out of the top of the costume stood two stars on long springs. Juliana exploded into fits of giggles, and between gulps explained the photo to Sophie, who shone the flashlight on it and held it closer to her eyes. She started laughing, too.

A voice came from behind them. "What on earth...?"

Juliana and Sophie turned around, their faces streaked with tears, to find Mom and Aunt Anne staring at them. Only now did Juliana really look at her surroundings: boxes of fabric, old board games, clothing, and rags lay all over the floor of the small laundry room.

"Juliana Elizabeth, you must tell me what's going on." Mom's voice was stern, her arms crossed. "And how you got your poor cousin involved."

Aunt Anne placed her hands on her hips and sighed.

"I'm sorry. I really tried to keep her from coming down. But we could hear the two of you laughing like hyenas, and when Scott told us that Sophie had told him to lie to me, Katy stormed down here."

Mom furrowed her brow. "You tried to keep me upstairs?"

The stairs creaked as Dad, Uncle Peter, and Opa came down.

"I'm sorry," Juliana said to Mom. "I was looking for this." Wanting to protect Sophie and Scott, she passed Mom the photo. She'd have to figure out a different birthday gift now. "Opa told me about it before the competition, and then when you mentioned it afterwards, I wanted to find it and surprise you with it for your birthday." She didn't add "surprise party." "That's all. I asked Sophie to help me because she, you know, she knows everything here. I don't."

"Tata remembered...?" Mom took the photo out of Juliana's hand. After a moment, she covered her mouth, and her eyes welled up. Juliana wanted to look away—parents weren't supposed to cry—but she didn't want to be rude.

"Oh my god...you found it..." Mom said. Dad wrapped his arm around her waist and smiled. "I...I was certain Anne had taken it at some point."

Aunt Anne smiled. "I have to confess, I wanted to. I was

going to show it to your friends, but after seeing how humiliated you felt, I couldn't."

Mom smiled. "That was even too mean for you."

"But Juliana, where did you find it? I really thought your mom had torn it up."

Sophie held up the tattered *Frustration* box.

"No way!" Uncle Peter said. He took it out of her hands and turned it around, inspecting it from all sides. "Now I remember!" All eyes fell on him. "All I heard through my door was the two of them arguing. I thought it had something to do with this photo." He passed the game to Juliana and then held out his hand to Mom for the photo. She gave it to him. "Yes, that's right. I was always jealous that the two of you got to dance. I think by now Anne had stopped, but Katy still got to. I thought this was the coolest costume, but the two of you were arguing about it, so I hid it so you wouldn't argue about it again."

Mom ruffled Uncle Peter's mullet and he playfully complained and then tried to re-spike his hair. Juliana giggled, and Sophie seemed to notice it, too. "You always were the peacemaker between us, weren't you?" Mom said.

Uncle Peter returned the photo to Mom. "You've got one smart, persistent girl here."

"With a really cool sidekick!" Juliana added.

Aunt Anne smiled and playfully said, "Who skipped some of her homework."

"You said it was okay to be Nancy Drew," Sophie shot back.

Aunt Anne leaned over to Mom. "Be careful what you say to your kids. They actually listen sometimes."

Uncle Peter asked, "But how did you figure it out?"

The eyes of all three Schuhmacher siblings were now on Juliana and Sophie.

Juliana blushed. "Well, you kept saying you loved board games, especially *Frustration*. And Opa told me about the photo and was certain it existed. Sophie and I had looked down here before, so I knew board games were in this closet, but I didn't think at the time that a random picture would be in one." She took a breath. "It was honestly just upstairs, when Mom mentioned the photo, and then the argument. I realized that Uncle Peter always tries to make everyone feel happy. If you guys were arguing about this picture, and he wanted to make you feel happy, he might have hidden it somewhere. He loves *Frustration*, and this hiding spot is really tight. You have to be small to get in there." She pointed to the closet. "I'll clean it up. I promise," she said.

Uncle Peter whistled. "Definitely a chip off the old block. Your mom loved reading mysteries when she was young."

Juliana looked sheepish. "Actually, I hate them. They're so frustrating."

Everyone groaned at the accidental bad pun.

Mom sort of hiccupped, then began to giggle. Within moments, her giggles turned into full belly laughs. "I...I... hated this photo," she blurted out. "My lord, I look ridiculous!" She held the photo for all to see.

Relief washed over Juliana. It sounded like she had been forgiven. But one detail was missing in her mind.

"Uncle Peter, if you loved *Frustration* so much, why did you hide the picture in here? I'm surprised no one found it."

"That was the old box," Aunt Anne explained. "Peter hated it. By the time he would've hidden this, Modr and Tata would've bought the new one—the one he uses now—because otherwise the family couldn't play without Peter crying about it."

"It was cracked and wrinkly!" Peter protested. "I always liked things smooth and shiny."

Everyone laughed.

Mom gave Juliana a tight hug while everyone else returned upstairs, including Sophie.

"Thank you," Mom said. "I'm so glad you found it."

"But why was this so important? I mean, it's just a costume."

Mom stared at the photo again. "It's perspective, Jules. I couldn't see the big picture at that age. I've been really struggling with this move, trying to figure out if it was the right decision or not, especially because of what you've gone through. But this is something I need to do and that I need to ask of you and your father. The big picture is that I need my family...before they disappear, like Modr already has."

Tears welled up in Mom's eyes again, and Juliana didn't know what to do. Parents were supposed to know what to do in all situations, to take control and fix every problem. Above all, they could only be happy, angry, bored, or disappointed. But not sad.

Yet here was Mom, crying for the second time in maybe fifteen minutes. The first time she'd cried out of happiness, and now she was crying out of sadness. She was regretting a decision she had made a long time ago, just like Uncle Peter had said. This was bigger than forgetting your tap shoes for your first practice, or not knowing anyone in town. This was wishing you could redo something you couldn't.

"Well, to be honest," Juliana said, "I'm kind of glad we came."

The smile on Mom's face told Juliana she had just given her mother her birthday gift.

CHAPTER SIXTEEN

lisabeth entered the kitchen, a round of cheese in her hand. The smell of a cigarette wafted through the house. Georg had arrived about five minutes before. Elisabeth had just called Mammi and now wanted to prepare some food for everyone. Not only was it polite to offer food to a guest, but Elisabeth secretly hoped it would bring her three siblings off the bed where they had huddled together. She had to somehow help them get used to Georg. Even if Mammi refused his offer, Elisabeth knew that he would help where he could anyway.

"Mammi's just finishing up something," Elisabeth said, "so she'll be here soon." She noticed he had a bowl for his ashes. "I'm sorry. I didn't think to ask before. Did you have to help yourself?"

He tapped the cigarette on the side of the bowl. "Rosina brought it to me," he said.

Surprised, Elisabeth gave her youngest sister a look of approval, and Rosina raised her chin in pride. Maybe spending time out on the *salasch* had helped her get used to Georg. Would that spread to the other siblings? But when Georg turned around to face Rosina, she grabbed on even tighter to Anna.

Maybe not.

Elisabeth asked Georg if he wanted anything to drink, but he declined. She returned to the kitchen and began slicing cheese. She reached for a normal plate from the cabinet and then stopped. *This has to be special,* she thought. Mammi might accept his help, even though she can't forgive him. Instead of a normal serving plate, Elisabeth pulled out a glass cake platter with floral etchings in it. Tata had had it specially ordered from Arad and had given it to Mammi as a gift at their first Christmas together. Now he wanted Mammi to accept help from his family. It seemed like an appropriate serving platter for cheese and bread.

As she cut away, Elisabeth peeked into the room and considered her poor siblings: should she put them out of their misery and suggest they go outside to play? When she noticed their unfinished homework on the table, though, she knew the answer. Maybe assign them some extra chores? They'd do them eagerly if it meant being excused out of the room. *Oh...wait a moment*, she thought as an idea formed in her mind.

She carried the serving platter, now beautifully decorated with white bread, cream-coloured cheese, and in the middle a bowl of butter, into the front room and set it on the table. She offered Georg some but he again declined.

"I'd like to speak with your mother first," he said, taking another puff on his cigarette. "But thank you."

"Of course." Elisabeth crossed her arms, attempting to take up a posture of authority. Now was a perfect time to try out her idea. "Georg, if you knew someone was lying to you, what would you do?" He blew out a mouthful of smoke and looked confused, so Elisabeth asked the question a different way. "If a child lied to you, maybe by not telling you where he had hidden something, what would you do?"

He nodded. Now he understood and Elisabeth fought to control the giddiness rising inside her. He set his cigarette in the bowl and turned around to face the children.

Luki jumped off the bed before Georg said a word. "It was me!" He darted out of the room so fast that Elisabeth burst out laughing. Why hadn't she thought of this method before? She looked up at the crucifix and laughed at the funny answer to her prayer.

"Luki! Show your mother respect!" Mammi shouted as

he rushed by her, almost knocking her over. She closed the door after him and entered the front room.

Georg stood up and nodded. "Good day, Lissa-Néni," he said to his aunt.

It was the first time Elisabeth had heard him greet someone. *He's really trying*, she realized.

"Georg," Mammi replied, her face hard as stone.

The two stared at each other for a moment: sorrow visible on Georg's face, scorn on Mammi's. The tension made the room uncomfortable for Elisabeth.

"Would anyone like something to drink?"

Georg shook his head and Mammi asked for water. Elisabeth's sisters still clung to each other and stared at their mother and cousin. They said nothing.

"I...also brought out cheese... in case someone's hungry," Elisabeth added, though she felt stupid stating the obvious. As she turned to get Mammi a glass of water, she saw Georg's eyes dart to Mammi's stomach. Did he know? *Of course he does, silly*, Elisabeth said to herself. *Eva's expecting a child, too.* It was something that was never openly talked about, and Mammi had made Elisabeth promise to never tell her siblings about the baby inside her.

Elisabeth returned with Mammi's water. Both she and Georg were still staring at each other as though each was waiting for the other to speak first.

"Bread? Cheese?" Elisabeth offered again.

Rosina inched her way off the bed, her eyes fixated on

Georg the entire time, as though expecting him to suddenly attack. She rushed around the other side of the table and sat down opposite him, her eyes still on him. But when she reached for a slice of cheese, Elisabeth admonished her. "Wait for our guest first!"

Georg broke eye contact with Mammi and gave Rosina a small smile. It was the first time Elisabeth had ever seen him smile without reacting to something so hilarious he couldn't help himself. Something had changed in him, but she couldn't figure out what.

"Go ahead," he said to Rosina.

Rosina shoved a piece of cheese in her mouth and then beckoned to Anna. "He can be really nice and not crazy!"

Elisabeth closed her eyes as her cheeks heated up. *Why me?* she asked Jesus.

Anna stayed put, shaking her head faster than a hummingbird's wings flapped.

Mammi spoke, ignoring her children. "I cannot forgive you for what you did to my brother."

Elisabeth jumped in. "But Mammi, he didn't—"

"Let your mother speak," Georg said.

Elisabeth's cheeks flushed anew.

"But I cannot ignore my situation," Mammi continued. "My children are too young to manage our land, we cannot afford day labourers, and my brother and brothers-in-law must look after their families." She crossed her arms over her chest. "I must ensure my children survive." She paused.

"I therefore accept your offer to farm our lands for one year only." Disdain on her face, she added, "Just so we understand each other, it humiliates me to accept it, and I dread what people will say about my family. But I have no other choice."

Elisabeth shot Mammi a look, but if Mammi saw it, she didn't let on. If Mammi's final comment convinced Georg to withdraw his offer, Elisabeth didn't know if she could forgive her for that. But to her surprise, Georg nodded and reached out his hand.

"It's unladylike to shake hands, Georg," Mammi said, keeping her arms crossed. "You should know that."

But Elisabeth could tell from the tone in Mammi's voice that that was not why she refused to shake his hand. Georg appeared to understand the meaning, too.

"Then it's agreed," he said. He sat down and took a slice of bread from the platter and buttered it.

"Yes," Mammi replied, also sitting and serving herself. "But Elisabeth cannot help you these next two days. She must study for her confirmation on Sunday."

Georg lay the butter knife back down on the glass platter. "It will be a big day for her. Samuel and I will finish planting the corn this coming week and the broom corn after Easter. Lissika and Rosina can help then."

Anna, who'd been staring at Georg this entire time, now followed Rosina as she inched her way to the table and sat down as far away from Georg as she could—which was only one chair over, around the corner from him. She reached for the cheese but then stopped herself.

"Would you like some cheese?" she asked Georg.

"Yes. Thank you, Anni," Georg replied and helped himself.

The house door opened and slammed shut.

"Here it is!" Luki said, running into the front room, holding up the magazine.

"My heavens, Luki! What happened to you!" Mammi cried out.

Luki was covered from head to toe in straw.

"What?" he asked. "Someone played with the hay. I had to crawl in to find this."

Elisabeth laughed, and everyone looked at her. "Nothing," she said. But she remembered Stefan feeding the animals when Maria had dropped by, looking for the magazine. He must have cleaned up a little in the barn, burying the magazine even more.

"Go back outside," Elisabeth said, "clean yourself off, and then you can sweep up after yourself."

"I'm not a girl!" he declared.

"Luki, listen to your sister," Georg said, and Luki sprinted out of the room.

CHAPTER SEVENTEEN

he lights flicked on.

"Surprise!"

Mom jumped and then promptly whacked Dad on the shoulder as smartphones recorded the entire scene. "I hate surprises and you purposely led me to one!"

"Just to see your face when it happened," he teased and kissed her on the cheek.

It reminded Juliana of when Rachel had helped Miss Kasia, her old dance teacher, organize a surprise goodbye party for Juliana in Calgary. Juliana hated surprises, too. The memory saddened her for a moment, but then another wet kiss between Dad and Mom drew her out of it. She wrinkled her nose. *Why?* she thought. She vowed she'd never act cutesy in front of people. It was just gross.

"Wow!" Mom exclaimed as she saw the table laden with

desserts. Her eyes got bigger and bigger. "Oh my god, Anne! You've outdone yourself! Black forest cake...*mandelkipfel*... are these *kwetscheknädel*?" Juliana had no idea what Mom was saying. Whatever that last one was, it looked like nothing more than balls of dough with something crumbly on top.

Mom stopped at one particular cake, decked out in white cream. She touched the glass platter it sat on, and Juliana could make out some etchings in it.

"This isn't Tata's cake platter, is it?" she asked. Aunt Anne nodded. Mom touched her hand to her heart.

Juliana had no idea what the big deal was about a glass platter. *Looks pretty kitschy,* she thought. *Like something you'd buy at a garage sale with those board games.*

Only after looking at all the desserts did Mom notice all the people, including old friends. Mom was all smiles. Even Tanya had come and was chatting with a few other women. Former dancers maybe? Mom did some awkward balancés over to them, gave them huge hugs, and began talking. All in all, about thirty people were celebrating in the Morgan house.

As she continued scanning the room and watching everyone talk to one another like old friends, Juliana saw Sophie sitting in the reading nook by herself. Juliana thought back to that night at Uncle Peter's when she was having a ton of fun and Sophie wasn't. She wouldn't let that happen again. As she made her way over, she noticed that the bookshelf where Sophie was sitting was filled with really thick books. With all the focus on photos, she'd never bothered to really look at the other books.

"Juliana!" Mom shouted through the room. "Come here! I want to introduce you to a few people!"

Juliana rolled her eyes. What was the point of meeting complete strangers she'd never otherwise talk to? Couldn't Mom see that Sophie was alone? But after Mom called her again, Juliana knew she had to obey. She didn't want to look like an idiot like she had at Christmas, especially not at her mom's surprise party. As Juliana crossed the room, though, Rebecca moved toward her younger sister. Juliana became worried. What was Rebecca going to tell Sophie now? Whatever it was, it would probably make her feel even worse.

Once Juliana reached Mom and her friends, she pasted on a stage smile.

"Juliana, you remember Tanya, right? And this is..." Juliana didn't hear the rest. She could see Rebecca and Sophie out of the corner of her eye. Rebecca leaned toward Sophie, and Sophie leaned away from Rebecca. Rebecca put her hand on the arm of the chair Sophie was sitting in, and Sophie looked in the other direction. Juliana could hear their voices, but she stood too far away to hear specific words.

"And this is..." Mom continued.

Juliana nodded but she was ignoring the rest of the

conversation she was supposed to be a part of and instead strained her ear to hear what Rebecca was saying to Sophie.

"Juliana?" Mom asked.

"Nice to meet you," Juliana replied and left Mom and her friends.

"Sorry," Juliana heard Mom say, slightly flustered. "She's, uh, she likes to hang out with Sophie."

"Oh, how lovely," a friend replied. "I'm sure that poor girl has a hard time making friends now. Did you know? I heard about this cure..."

Keep moving, Juliana thought. *Don't look back.* As Juliana finally reached Sophie and her sister, Rebecca said, "Fine, be that way." She turned around, rolled her eyes at Juliana, and said, "At some point in time, she's got to accept what she has."

Juliana didn't even bother to watch where Rebecca was headed. Sophie looked too upset.

"Hey," Juliana said and sat next to Sophie on the couch. "You okay?"

Sophie shrugged and stared at the floor.

"Anything I can help with?"

"No."

After a few moments of silence, Juliana pulled one of the thick books off the shelves so she could pretend to read it. She almost dropped it because of its weight. *Nancy Drew. Might as well see what these are like*, she thought. When she opened it, though, her cheeks burned. It was large print. Very large print. These were Sophie's books. Should Juliana continue to pretend to read them now? She didn't want to hurt Sophie's feelings more.

"It's okay," Sophie said. "You can put it back. You'll look stupid reading it. Mom bought me some of her favourite books in large print once we got the diagnosis. It was supposed to make me feel better."

"I'm...I'm sorry."

"Stop it with the apologizing," Sophie said. "I hate it."

Juliana placed the book back on the shelf. She vowed to say nothing more until Sophie spoke. Maybe all Sophie wanted was someone to listen to her. *Like what Rachel needed when her mom died*, she thought. She silently thanked Shawna, one of her high school friends, for that advice.

Uncle Peter laughed out loud at something and Brian patted him on the back in approval. Everyone around them laughed, too. Opa was talking to a man his age. Dad had said Karl, the friend Opa had gone to Cuba with, would come, so that could be him. Scott was running through the room with his superhero figures while Dean was chasing him. Charlie and Tony were staring at something on a phone and laughing. Rebecca was talking to some of the adults.

Why was no one paying attention to Sophie? But by the same token, what was Juliana supposed to do now? Sophie was still upset over whatever Rebecca had said and she didn't seem to want to do anything. Should Juliana just leave her alone? Juliana sometimes liked being left alone. Maybe it was best to just ask? Or would that offend her younger cousin? *I suppose the only way I can stop guessing is to ask*, she decided.

"Do you want me to go? I can't tell if you want to be left alone. But if you do, just tell me."

"I hate large groups," Sophie said, not really answering Juliana's question.

"Oh." What else could Juliana say? She loved performing in front of large groups—the more people the better. She didn't like being a stranger in a large room full of people, but Sophie wasn't a stranger here. Juliana couldn't figure out what was bothering her. Her cousin was normally cheery and comfortable with family.

"What did Rebecca tell you? It looked pretty bad." Sophie shrugged, so Juliana tried something else. "You helped me deal with Rachel's mom's death. Maybe I can help you with this?"

Sophie seemed to mull it over for a few seconds, and then began to speak, still staring at the floor. "I know everyone here is looking at me, thinking, 'Oh, that poor girl. She's going blind.' So they just avoid me. Easier to not talk to me than have to learn how to talk with me." A knot formed in Juliana's stomach and her cheeks burned. She had been like that, too, when she first met Sophie.

Sophie turned to face Juliana and sighed. "My sister's had it easy all these years: good grades, popular, athletic... and she can read whatever she wants to. She's never had to work for anything." Her lips tightened. "I saw the ophthalmologist two weeks ago. He said I had to make sure to wear my sunglasses often or my eyes could get worse faster." She sniffled. "And then he gave me these special glasses."

So far, Juliana was trying to figure out what was so upsetting. How could sunglasses and special glasses that helped Sophie see better be a bad thing?

Sophie continued, "They're called bioptics and have these stupid tiny telescopes on them to help me see far away."

It clicked.

"You just want to look normal," Juliana said.

Sophie tried to swallow her tears. "Who wears sunglasses when it's overcast? Or telescopes on their glasses? Rebecca doesn't get it. She's been normal her whole life. She even looked beautiful in braces. She doesn't get it." Juliana scanned the room again and everyone still looked occupied. Juliana felt sadness for Sophie at the same time as she felt anger toward her cousin's family. But what could she do to help? Nothing. She couldn't very well tell Aunt Anne to pay more attention to Sophie, or yell at Rebecca to show her younger sister some understanding. *Just like I couldn't fly to be with Rachel*, she thought. But one thing Rachel used to do for

Juliana was lift her spirits, and maybe that's what Sophie needed right now.

"They're all old people talking about old-people stuff," she said. "There's nothing interesting here, anyway. How about some TV in the basement?"

A small smile crept on to Sophie's face and she nodded.

CHAPTER EIGHTEEN

*E*lisabeth was ecstatic. mammi had surprised her that morning by telling her that she had closed the workshop for today and tomorrow so Elisabeth could have two days away from her chores to study for her confirmation on Sunday. Elisabeth didn't even have to help with the big clean-up her sisters and Mammi had to do every Saturday.

She had chosen to settle with her books in the back room, away from the hustle and bustle of the household when the others were home. Several lanterns gave off more light and heat, and Luther's *Small Catechism*, the family Bible, and several books of Luther's teachings lay sprawled out on the otherwise empty dining room table.

What had her attention, though, was Tata's letter. Elisabeth had a lot to write him, though she knew now was not the time. Mammi would turn the colour of a beet if she saw Elisabeth writing—or drawing, for that matter—instead of studying. However, there was one thing Elisabeth could write in her letter that would not make Mammi angry. It was a necessary step in her confirmation: asking Tata for forgiveness. Pastor Fröhlich had talked with all the confirmands at their last lesson and emphasized repeatedly how crucial this step was to becoming adults in the church. Elisabeth knew she had to say it exactly as he had taught them.

She began to write.

Dear Tata,

My confirmation is on Sunday, as you know. And as you also know, I must ask you for forgiveness. I cannot do it in person, which makes me very sad, but at least I can do it in this letter.

Dearest Tata, because I have resolved to accept Holy Communion today for the very first time, I am reminded that I have sinned against God and against you and that I have sometimes deliberately and wantonly offended and angered you. Therefore, for Jesus's sake, I ask you to forgive me my missteps and sins. I promise also in the future to honour and love you, to observe the will of God and therefore to better my life. Amen.

Elisabeth re-read the passage and giggled. She added after that paragraph,

Well, I guess it is not today that I will receive Holy Communion for the first time but rather on Sunday. Can you forgive me that error, too?

Someone knocked at the side door.

"Why must people visit when I have so much to do?" Mammi grumbled as she dusted off her hands on her apron and opened the door.

Elisabeth craned her neck to see who it might be, but she recognized the voice instantly.

"Hello, Frau Schuhmacher. Is Lissika home?"

Elisabeth jumped off her chair. "Maria!" She ran out to the kitchen and embraced her best friend. Then she took a step back. "What...?" Maria's hair had been cut straight across her face.

"Do you like it?" Maria asked. "I almost cut off all my hair, but once the hairdresser held the scissors up, I couldn't do it. What's the point of a *haube* if you don't have hair to put under it? So it's just the front. They're called bangs."

"It's so modern! I love it!"

Mammi gave a disapproving look. "Useless. Now you have to cut those all the time like a man or your hair will eventually poke out your eyes." She shook her head. "We do things a certain way because it's practical to do so. There's no need to change them." She placed her hands on her lower back, something she seemed to be doing more of lately. "Elisabeth must study today and tomorrow. She has no time for visitors."

Maria's face turned red. "I'm sorry," she said. "I just wanted to bring Elisabeth this gift." She held up a lovely silver hair comb with floral etchings in it.

Elisabeth took the gift in her hands and marvelled at its beauty. "Oh, Maria! How can I ever repay you?"

"It's a gift, silly! You don't repay people for gifts!"

Elisabeth hugged her best friend. Maria took it out of Elisabeth's hands, gingerly removed the comb that held Elisabeth's braid in place at the top of her head, and slid the new one in.

"Perfect. Exactly where it looks becoming on you." Maria's smile told Elisabeth what her best friend meant: that it made her look attractive to Stefan.

"Also useless," Mammi said. "Now Lissika will constantly worry if she loses it."

"My braid would fall out," Elisabeth said matter-of-factly. "I would notice."

Mammi gave both girls a disapproving look and took a step toward the door. "Now, Maria, Elisabeth must study."

Maria nodded briskly and also stepped toward the door.

"Wait!" Elisabeth said. "Mammi, just one more minute." She ran to the front room and stretched to retrieve Maria's magazine from atop the cupboards. She opened the front cover, and it was still there: an apology from Luki.

"Here," she said as she gave it to Maria. "Luki had hidden it in the haystack by the horses. I think I got all the hay out of it."

Maria smiled as she accepted her magazine back. Elisabeth showed her Luki's letter.

Deer Maria,

I am sorry that I took your megazeen. I was jelus becaus evrewon was going to help Mammi mak nis shoes but Im the man of the house. It is my job to desid what gets mad.

From,

Luki

Maria laughed. "That is so sweet." She folded the note and slid it into her hand purse. She clapped her hands in excitement. "I found a lovely magazine from England in Arad that I really must show you! But next time, at my house!" The girls laughed together.

Mammi's eyes narrowed. "I did not close down my workshop today so Elisabeth could gossip."

Maria twisted her hands around her hand purse. Mammi could scare almost anyone. Elisabeth wondered if even Stefan could withstand Mammi's stares.

"I know, Frau Schuhmacher, and I'm really sorry. But I also wanted to ask you...implore you...to please reconsider about the shoes. We spent these past few days in Arad, and Mammi wanted me to have nice shoes for when the dances begin after Easter, but none of them fit me. My feet are wide, like a man's!" Maria's cheeks turned red. "Could you please make me a modern pair of shoes? Maybe just something with a little heel and...a more modern shape?"

Mammi sighed and glanced from one girl to the next. Even Elisabeth pleaded, but only with her eyes. She dared not say anything lest it unleash more of Mammi's anger.

Mammi nodded.

We did win the war, Elisabeth thought in astonishment.

Maria jumped up and down, clapping her hands again. "Thank you, Frau Schuhmacher!"

Mammi's face remained in its tight-lipped form. "Stop looking like a monkey," she told Maria. "Your mother would be embarrassed by such a show."

Elisabeth had to laugh—despite her mother's attempts at staying serious and not smiling, she could be quite funny.

"But it must wait until after Easter," Mammi said.

Maria nodded eagerly. "Oh!" She looked at the magazine and to Elisabeth's surprise, Maria handed it back. "Then you'll need to keep this a little longer: I'm certain you'll want to draw the shoes in your book before you return the magazine."

Maria thanked Mammi one more time, and she and Elisabeth kissed each other on the cheek. Elisabeth watched her best friend skip along the side of the house and through the gates.

"Elisabeth, either you return to your studies or begin baking for Sunday."

Elisabeth startled Mammi by kissing her on the cheek and then returned to her studies. The first thing she did after she sat down, though, was spend several minutes giving thanks to Jesus for His help.

THE SUN HADN'T YET RISEN, BUT ELISABETH COULDN'T SLEEP. Not only was it Palm Sunday, but the scents of Mammi's baking from the day before still filled the house. Elisabeth couldn't wait to feast that afternoon.

Sitting in the kitchen, she looked up at the crucifix above the door. The last few days had truly been miraculous: Mammi had accepted Georg's offer to farm their fields and Stefan's to build a stove, and she had agreed to make new shoes for Maria.

"You do work in miracles, don't You?" she said to Jesus.

She adjusted the angle of her drawing book and shaded in the heel of the fourth shoe she was copying from Maria's magazine. She wanted to give the magazine back to Maria as soon as possible.

Elisabeth heard the door to the front room open, and Mammi stumbled into the kitchen, just waking up. She rubbed her eyes and then her back. Expecting a baby looked painful to Elisabeth.

Elisabeth closed her drawing book and offered Mammi a cup of tea or water.

"No," Mammi said. She yawned, rubbed her eyes again, and then looked sternly at Elisabeth. "Today is your special day. It is your last day as a child in this family. *I* will look after you."

Elisabeth smiled and recited the request for forgiveness.

Mammi patted Elisabeth on the head and kissed her on the cheek. "Yes, I forgive you. Now, let us get your dress out of the closet and begin getting ready. Use the back room for now—today will be a busy day, so we will let Luki and your sisters sleep."

Elisabeth's insides tumbled around with more emotions than she believed she could hold at one time: joy at the help Mammi had accepted from Tata's family, eagerness because of Mammi's willingness to try making new shoes, excitement because Elisabeth would finally become an adult in the church today and sit up at the front with Maria, but also sadness because Tata would not be there to see his eldest daughter celebrate such an important event.

Mammi opened one of the wardrobes in the back room and gingerly lifted out Elisabeth's Sunday clothes and laid them over the feather blankets and pillows that were stacked high on the guest bed: a white blouse with white satin ribbons down the front, next to the buttons, and a flowing embroidery pattern—also stitched in white—followed next to the ribbon. The white, narrow sleeves puffed slightly at the shoulder and ended in lovely lace cuffs. Every pleat on the white skirt was perfectly pressed, and the dark blue apron didn't even have folds in it. When had Mammi had time to do this without Elisabeth knowing? *Probably when I was out at the* salasch, Elisabeth realized. She knew Mammi would prepare the dress, but given that she was carrying a baby and trying to run Tata's shoemaking business, Elisabeth hadn't expected that much would be done.

"You've even starched the underskirts," Elisabeth said.

Mammi placed her hands on her hips. "Do you really believe I would have my daughter walk down the aisle looking flat?" Then Mammi opened a drawer and lifted out a few shawls. Elisabeth assumed Mammi was simply going to let her choose which shawl she wanted today, but then Mammi pulled out a shawl she had never seen before. Elisabeth's heart got stuck in her throat as Mammi unfolded it: It was green cashmere and had been embroidered in colourful, delicate floral patterns.

"Omama made this," Mammi said, meaning her mother, "especially for you."

Omama was cranky, mean, and strict. That she could produce something so light and beautiful did not fit Elisabeth's image of her.

Mammi gingerly lifted out a little, white handkerchief from the drawer next. Elisabeth immediately recognized it as the one Anna had been working on for the past two weeks. Now she felt guilty for assuming Anna had stolen the magazine. Elisabeth took it out of Mammi's hands, and as she inspected Anna's work, Mammi carried in the washing bowl and a towel. Elisabeth lay the handkerchief over the back of a chair.

"I'll prepare breakfast," Mammi said. "You wash yourself up." After warning Elisabeth to not splash a drop of water anywhere—this was the room they would use for entertaining the family members who would be joining them for lunch after church, she closed the door. Elisabeth dunked the cloth into the cold water and began washing her face.

Mammi had cooked a simple breakfast so everyone could eat and clean up quickly. She had then disappeared into the back room to get dressed.

Elisabeth had moved to the front room, now that her siblings were ready for church. She hadn't wanted to brush her long, blonde hair in the back room and have to clean hair off the floor.

"May I?" Anna asked as Elisabeth began undoing her own braid from last night. Before Elisabeth could even say yes, Anna had turned a chair around and positioned it behind Elisabeth so she could reach her older sister's hair more easily.

Luki came rushing in. "I almost forgot! Your shoes!" he said. "I cleaned them for you!"

"Thank you," Elisabeth replied and inspected the black satin slippers while Anna tugged at her hair with the brush. "You've done a very good job, Luki. Tata would be proud of you." She smiled at him, though she couldn't really turn her head. But she did see him lift his chin and push out his tiny chest.

"I'm going to hold this for you," Rosina said as she picked up a white, beaded hairband that Elisabeth would wear.

Elisabeth had to smile. There was no need for Rosina to do anything—the hairband was fine on the table as it was —but she understood Rosina's desire to help.

"I'm so grateful that you're all helping me," she said. "And most of all, I'm grateful that I have all of you."

As Anna braided her hair, Elisabeth recited her favourite prayer in her mind, the Our Father. She paused at the fifth petition, *And forgive us our trespasses, as we forgive those who trespass against us.* After all her studying, she could recite the petition's meaning by heart and did so aloud: "This means that we pray in this petition that our Father in heaven would not look upon our sins, nor on their account deny our prayer; for we are worthy of none of the things for which we pray, neither have we deserved them; but that He would grant them all to us by grace; for we daily sin much and indeed deserve nothing but punishment: so will we also heartily forgive and readily do good to those who sin against us."

Anna tied a ribbon at the bottom of Elisabeth's braid and left it down for the hairband, which Rosina passed to Elisabeth.

"What does that mean?" Rosina asked.

Elisabeth placed the hairband on her head and Anna tied it closed in the back, underneath the braid. Elisabeth looked at herself squarely in the looking glass. "We're all sinners, Rosina. We all make mistakes. That's why, when we pray to God for help, we hope He looks past our sins and grants us our prayers. But because we hope for that, we must also forgive others who have wronged us."

Luki scratched his ear. "Does that mean you forgive me for taking the magazine?"

Fully dressed now, Elisabeth bent down and hugged her little brother. "Of course, I do!" She hugged and forgave Anna and Rosina, too, and asked them to forgive her for suspecting them.

The door to the back room opened, and Mammi stepped out, covered from head to toe in black: a black headscarf tied under her chin, her black *tschurak* over her bodice, her black skirt atop several white underskirts, a black apron over her overskirt, and black shoes. The only colour was her socks: horizontally striped blue and white. *She looks so elegant*, Elisabeth thought. Mammi's skirts floated out even wider than Elisabeth's, and Elisabeth couldn't wait until she was old enough to dress like that.

"Everyone, get your shoes on," Mammi instructed. She studied Elisabeth. Elisabeth looked down the front of her dress, too. Her four underskirts pushed her white, pleated overskirt out far, giving her thin figure a fuller shape. *Will Stefan like this?* she wondered and then admonished herself for thinking about him when she should have been thinking about Jesus. She again fingered the delicate lace on her cuff and gently brushed her hand down the white buttons on her blouse.

She couldn't help herself and asked Mammi, "I look beautiful, don't I?"

Mammi blinked a few times and swallowed, and Elisabeth wondered if Mammi was trying to hold back tears.

"Are you ready?" Mammi asked.

Elisabeth turned to face herself in the looking glass. Was she ready? She had studied fervently, and she believed she could answer any questions about the catechism and Bible that Pastor Fröhlich would ask her. Her stomach churned out of nervousness, but a deeper sensation threatened to push through, a mixture of fear and disgust. Not only did she have to ask her godparents for their forgiveness, she had to promise to love and honour them.

"Elisabeth?" Mammi called and returned to the front room. "What is it?"

"I don't know if I can promise to love and honour my godparents."

Mammi stepped behind Elisabeth, placed her hands on her daughter's shoulders, and looked at her through the looking glass. Her face turned solemn.

"This is difficult but if you do not find a way to make this right within yourself, you will not be confirmed and you will not be allowed to marry."

Mammi left Elisabeth alone while she retrieved a thick, black shawl for herself from the back room and Elisabeth's new one from Omama.

"Come," she said, standing at the house door. "If we do not leave now so you can visit Konrad and Margarethe and ask them for forgiveness, we will be late for your confirmation." She held out Elisabeth's shawl.

Elisabeth slipped into her black, satin dress slippers and joined her family in the kitchen. She placed her shawl behind her neck, pulled it over her shoulders, and crossed the ends over her chest and tied them together at her back.

Jesus, You will help me, won't You? she asked silently as the family headed out the door.

CHAPTER NINETEEN

"Oh my god!" Sophie said, almost choking as she laughed. "That was...that was..." She couldn't finish her sentence, and it didn't matter. Juliana was laughing so hard she could hardly hear her. The singing competition had included a horrible singer who was so full of herself that they'd clearly brought her on only for laughs.

"She sounded like cats fighting!" Sophie finally blurted out. Juliana snorted, and Sophie laughed even louder.

"Stop it!" Juliana said through her tears. "I...I can't take it anymore!" She was crying.

The show cut to commercial, and it gave the girls a few minutes to calm down. Between singing acts, Juliana had told Sophie more about Omama's book of drawings and how it was like a photo album but in pencil.

The show returned from commercial and spotlighted a balding man dressed in a hoodie, holding a baby boy on his lap.

"Oh, lord," Juliana said. "The sob story."

"Yuck."

The girls chuckled as the man talked about how he couldn't wait for his son to see him on television, to see him realizing his dream, of finally making it in showbiz.

"He doesn't care!" Juliana shouted at the screen. "He's a baby!"

"Get to the singing already!" Sophie added.

As he droned on and soggy music played in the background, Sophie asked, "Can you tell me more about the drawings?"

Juliana smiled. "So long as you wash the lettuce at my house." Sophie held out her hand and they shook on it. "Listen, let me get something," Juliana said. "I found something in the dungeon the other night when I went snooping again. I wanted to see if I could find any more letters but I found this instead. I'll be right back."

She ran upstairs, did her best to hide from the adults, grabbed her backpack, and brought it back downstairs. She unzipped the laptop compartment and pulled out an ancient copy of *Vanity Fair* magazine that had a red cover and a drawing on the front. The drawing was of two men in the bottom right, one dressed more formally than the other, and the bottom half of a woman in the top left corner, holding a leash with a dog in the middle.

"I didn't now if I'd get a chance to show it to you tonight. It's from 1919," Juliana said.

"Whoa…" Sophie said as she brushed her hand up and down it. "And the cover is so bright and big, I can see most of it."

"You have to see this page," Juliana said and opened the magazine to a page that had four women golfers photographed. "I mean, check out those sexy pants!"

To her delight, the pictures were big enough that Sophie could at least see what Juliana was talking about.

As they continued to flip through the magazine, Juliana realized that Sophie was becoming a bit like a sister to her. They hung out together, talked a lot, watched TV together. They'd even sort of argued already. That's what sisters did, right?

"Did Omama draw anything like this?" Sophie asked as she closed the magazine.

"I looked last night, and the next few drawings are of shoes. Her parents were shoemakers, Opa said once. But I don't know if she drew the shoes because she liked them or because she wanted to make them."

"Maybe they were her favourite shoes. How many did she draw?"

Juliana thought for a moment. "Four, I think. They were all different women's shoes."

"Maybe she loved shoes and had a closet full?"

Sophie held the magazine closer to her face as she perused more of the drawings. Juliana felt a warmth inside her growing. Jasmine at the dance studio, Meghan and Shawna at school, and now Sophie in her own family. Juliana had been sad when she realized that Rachel had other friends to help her through her mom's death. But now Juliana understood what having different friends felt like, too, and it made her happy.

Dripping in sweat, Juliana slid her tap board under the basement couch and untied her tap shoes. During this afternoon's practice session, she had focused on a few points the judges had called her on at the last competition.

"At the very least, I don't want judges mentioning those mistakes again," she said to herself as she wiped the sweat off her brow.

Next on her plan: stretching. After a tap practice session, Juliana's muscles were warm enough that she could get some serious length out of them. She sat on the carpet and spread her legs into a wide straddle on the floor. She smiled in satisfaction when her legs stopped an inch farther back than they normally did at the start of straddle. Taking in a deep breath, Juliana reached her left arm above her head and then bent her upper body over her right leg, exhaling along the way.

Someone knocked on the side door upstairs, and Juliana heard Opa's steps as he ascended the stairs and answered. She inhaled again and then tried to reach even farther as she exhaled.

"Yulika!" Opa called. "Sophie's here!"

"Tell her to come down!" Juliana replied and within twenty seconds, her cousin appeared in the doorway.

"I got bored at home, so I thought I'd see what you're up to," Sophie asked.

"Actually, I was planning to stretch for a while. But if you're okay with my doing that, stay! Nothing says I can't talk."

"Cool."

Opa followed a moment later. *Looks like I'll have an audience*, Juliana thought, but she didn't mind. With the photo now found and given—Mom had framed it and taken it with her to work—Juliana had to return to her regular schedule. If she could socialize with family while doing so, then double bonus.

"Doesn't that hurt?" Opa asked, his face contorted in a look of pain.

"A little," Juliana replied from her horizontal position. "But not much. It just takes practice."

She switched arms and stretched to the other side.

"It was so nice to see all my family this week," Opa said.

"And now to see the two of you. I knew before you came, Yulika, that you and Sophie would be like friends."

Both girls blushed as they looked at each other, and Opa sat down in the armchair. He invited Sophie to sit on the couch, and Juliana turned around to face them. Returning her legs to straddle, she now faced the leg she was bending over, reaching under her foot with the opposite arm.

"Opa," she said, facing her knee, "I showed Sophie Omama's book of drawings. Your grandparents were shoemakers, right?"

"Yes. It was funny because *Schuhmacher* is German for *shoemaker*."

Sophie cocked her head to the side. "So the last name was chosen because of their profession?"

Opa shook his head, and Juliana couldn't tell if Sophie had seen that or not. *Probably not*, she thought. He answered, "Opa's father was a blacksmith. Before that, I don't know. Probably farmers. But Opa was the first shoemaker in the family in Semlak. We came from Germany. I guess someone a long time ago was a shoemaker, too."

Juliana sat up. "I looked at Omama's book last night, and she drew shoes on several pages. Did she make shoes, too?" She switched sides again and folded herself down over her other leg.

"No," Opa replied. "She never learned. But she drew

those so Omama could copy them and make fancier shoes for the richer people in the village."

"So it wasn't because she loved shoes?" Sophie said. "I thought maybe she had a closet full of them or something."

Opa laughed. "No, no, Sophie. Your Omama back then would have had maybe two pairs of slippers—one out of satin for dressy occasions and one out of leather for in the house and outside—and a pair of boots."

Juliana laughed. "I have more shoes than that in my dance bag alone!"

Sophie asked, "Who did she make shoes for then?"

A sudden cloud came over Opa's face. "Georg was Oma's first customer for the new shoes. He bought them for his wife." He paused and his eyes became unfocused. Juliana had seen this look before, the day Opa had thought she needed to start looking for a husband because she was fourteen.

"Mammi, you have to stop being nice to him," he said.

Juliana glanced at Sophie, who was looking from Opa to Juliana and back. *She probably doesn't see what's happening*, Juliana thought.

"He doesn't look after his family," Opa said.

"Who?" Sophie asked.

"You know who I mean," Opa said, impatience filling his voice. "You have to stop helping him."

Juliana scrambled to sit next to Sophie.

"He's seeing things," she whispered. "It's not you."

Quiet panic appeared on Sophie's face and Juliana placed a hand of comfort on her cousin's shoulder.

"Mammi, I said stop helping him! He doesn't care about his family!"

Juliana didn't want to leave Sophie alone with Opa while she went to get help. His behaviour clearly frightened her, and Juliana didn't know if this episode would end soon or continue. She also didn't want to leave him alone—she didn't know what he would do if the girls suddenly left. Mom was out running errands, but Dad was sleeping upstairs to prepare for another long week of driving. *If this ends before I wake Dad, though, then Dad won't be rested for the road,* she thought. After Rachel's mom had died in a car crash, Juliana often worried about Dad's safety, even though he was the one in the tractor trailer.

Wait—Dad had once brought Opa out of this by talking with him. Can I do that, too? she thought. She had to try— she only hoped it wouldn't anger Opa any further.

"Opa? Where are you?" she asked.

"We're at home," he replied. "Can't you see that?"

"Where's home?"

"Are you all right, Mammi?" Opa asked. He stepped toward the girls. Juliana's palms began to sweat. "We're home. Your bed is just over there in the corner." Opa pointed toward the television. "Maybe you should rest."

Sophie's shoulders almost reached her ears and tears welled up in her eyes. She obviously hadn't seen Opa act like this before. Juliana had to think fast. He could see them and hear them, but he was in another world, and this time, the sound of someone's voice wasn't bringing him out of it.

Like a gift from the gods, her phone rang. Juliana ran over to her practice area and picked it up off the floor.

Opa panicked. "Mammi? What is that?" He stared at the phone.

"It's a telephone, Opa," Juliana said. She glanced at the caller ID. Mom! She swiped right to answer and passed it to Opa. "It's for you. It's your daughter, Katy."

Opa placed the phone to his ear. "Who is this? I don't have a daughter."

Juliana couldn't hear what Mom said, but within two minutes, Opa had returned to reality.

"No, Katy, everything's fine," he said, but Juliana could see his whole face and even his ears turn red. "Yes, yes, everything's fine. Um…" He rubbed his nose and gave the girls embarrassed glances. Then his eyes lit up. "Thank you! How could I forget? The German hour!" Without saying goodbye, he handed the phone back to Juliana. "I don't know how to hang that up," he said and hustled out of the room and up the stairs as fast as his seventy-year-old legs could carry him.

Juliana put the phone on speaker.

"Mom? You're on speaker. Sophie's here, too. Opa's upstairs."

"Are you girls okay? I called just to ask what I can bring home for supper tonight. What happened there?"

Sophie had relaxed again, and Juliana explained Opa's hallucination.

"It was scary, Aunt Katy," Sophie added.

"I'm sure it was," Mom replied. "I'm sorry you had to see that. Was he angry?"

"No," Juliana answered, trying to sound confident for Sophie. "Just really confused. He thought we were his mom." But inside she was scared, too. What if Mom hadn't called? She didn't know if Opa would've panicked if Juliana had left the room or if he may have even tried to lay Sophie down in the corner, on top of the television.

"I don't know if this will help," Mom said, "but he only seems to have these maybe once a month right now or so. I'm sorry it happened while I was out. Maybe I'll talk to his doctor—maybe something in his medication needs to change. And I wonder if it would be good for you to talk with a counselor about all this, Jules? I can arrange for an appointment. I'll take off work if I have to and come with you. But they know how to help. Sophie, you can come, too, if your mom says it's okay."

Sophie glanced at Juliana. "Yeah, Aunt Katy, that would be good."

"I'll call your mom now and then call a counselor first thing in the morning."

Mom took Juliana's supper request—quinoa chicken salad from the deli—and hung up.

"You okay?" Juliana asked Sophie.

"Yeah. You?"

"I think so."

A moment of silence passed.

"Do you think he's scared, too?" Sophie asked.

"Yeah, I do," Juliana replied.

Juliana thought back to Omama's book. She'd have to start asking him about those drawings now, every day if necessary. Time was running out.

SETTING THE RECORD STRAIGHT

Between Worlds tells a fictional contemporary story together with a story that is historical fiction. In both parts of the book, I've taken facts about life in that time and included them in a fictional story. In writing novels, the story always comes first (because otherwise this would be a history textbook), so this section explains any important facts that may have been changed to fit the story and adds more background to the story. If you have any questions about what you've read in this or any of the other books in the series, ask away! My contact information is in the "Stay in Touch!" section.

PREPARATION FOR EASTER IN SEMLAK

Elisabeth's family is Lutheran, which is one branch of Christianity. Easter marks the defining celebration in Christianity: the death and resurrection of Christ. To be Christian is to believe in Jesus's resurrection.

Just over forty days before Easter is Ash Wednesday. This day marks the beginning of Lent and symbolizes the forty days Jesus spent in the desert, where the devil tempted him three times. Despite his exhaustion and plausible delirium, Jesus rejected the devil each time. Today, it is common for Christians to take on some form of fasting during this time. For the Lutherans in Semlak, families practised a variety of fasting rituals, but usually only during the week between Palm Sunday and Easter. For example, on Thursday, which was known as "Green Thursday," many would eat something green, like spinach. On Good Friday, when Jesus's death is mourned, they would not eat any meat. Catholics, by contrast, usually take up some form of fasting for the entire Lenten period, and many will not eat meat on each Friday during Lent. I remember in my youth once promising to not eat any chocolate for the entire Lenten period. (I think I forgot twice.)

If you've read anything about Germany, you've likely read about Fasching, a time of celebration before Lent and its forty days of fasting. However, because Martin Luther

removed the requirement to fast, which Catholics practised, celebrating Fasching no longer made sense to
Lutherans. So that's why you haven't read about it in this
series.

In Elisabeth's congregation, the time before Easter was
also used for spring cleaning. However, this was more than
just getting into the corners and wiping out old spiderwebs;
it involved repainting the entire house in limewash. As you
may have noticed, this was women's work. Men would have
helped with major repairs to the household, but women
looked after the upkeep.

FARMING PRACTICES

The hardest aspect to recreate in any historical fiction is
daily life. Add to this a society that didn't record their daily
routines, and you have an almost impossible task. The
Lutheran ancestors that founded the Lutheran church in
Semlak came from different areas than many of the
Catholic Germans around them. This led me to believe that
some of their farming practices may have differed from the
others. Many of these German towns had their own folk
costumes (called *tracht* in German) and regional dialects, so
it stood to reason that other ares of life differed from one
town to the next. However, the farmers could also only
work with what tools were available, and certainly the land
and climate would have also dictated aspects of farming

across regions such that many farmers used the same techniques.

I learned about the sack of seeds around the neck from my grandfather. Nick Tullius, a member of the Donauschwaben Villages Helping Hands, explained that one person made a hole for the corn kernels and the second person dropped a few in. However, when it came to planting wheat and other grains with small seeds, my grandfather and Anne Dreer, another member of the organization, explained how farmers would "broadcast" their seeds, i.e., throw them out in an arc with each step.

Machines already existed to help with this—a member of this cultural group told me her father was a mechanic and rented out in his village seed drills that were pulled by horses—but my general impression is that this availability depended on the village/town and the mindset of its people. The Germans in Semlak, for example, strike me as having been somewhat resistant to change, because most of them didn't connect to the village's electrical lines until the Communists forced them to twenty-five years after the line had been installed. Many of these Germans believed in the old adage, *If it ain't broke, don't fix it.* In other words, if the process they had developed worked, why change? Given how *fast* change happens today, I must admit that I find that adage appealing.

BOYS AND DANCE IN NORTH AMERICA

When I began writing this book, I wasn't sure if Uncle Peter also danced in his childhood or not: There's an old stereotype that all male dancers are gay, and I worried my readers might think I was just rehashing it. On the other hand, Uncle Peter is the youngest of three siblings, and because his older sisters danced (although Aunt Anne quit before she became a teenager), it seemed natural that he would have wanted to dance, as well.

Stereotype? Or natural character development?

The final straw that broke the camel's back, so to speak, was a story that went viral while I was writing this novel. It was about six-year-old Prince George in England. A host on a popular morning TV show had laughed at him for enjoying his ballet lessons. Within twenty-four hours, her comments had unleashed a fury within the dance world.

It also confirmed for me that many out there still believe that boys shouldn't dance, or if they do, that it should be some form of "masculine" dance. (Because the jumps and turns male ballet dancers do are not masculine? I know. Makes no sense to me, either.) That someone with such a powerful voice spread the message that ballet is not only boring but also not something for boys told me that ballet still hadn't broken the gender barrier.

So that's why Uncle Peter says in Chapter I that he wanted to dance as a kid but couldn't because of his gender.

In his generation, boys rarely danced because of gender norms. The TV controversy demonstrated to me that many out there today still believe boys shouldn't dance.

Boys are still heavily bullied for dancing, especially for studying ballet. If you know of any boy who is bullied at school (or even at home) for his artistic pursuits, be they dance or otherwise, show him your support and show others that you support him. The arts are how we express ourselves. For some of us, expressing ourselves means using twenty-six characters, as I do. For others, it involves thousands of colours and lines. For others still, it's the myriad ways our bodies can move, either on their own to dance, by using an instrument to create music, or both, for example, tap. Follow your own artistic passions, but help others follow theirs, too.

IF YOU HAVE AN EMBARRASSING DANCE COSTUME

Oh, man, I so get it. You want to look cool in front of your friends and then you get stuck with a costume you can't even look at yourself in. I've been Ernie's rubber ducky (age six), a card in *Alice in Wonderland* (maybe age eight?), and Rainbow Brite's sprite (age eleven, complete with white fur bag, stars on springs coming out of my head, and rainbow-striped leggings over my skinny legs). I'm sure there have been others I've since blocked out of my memory.

I once interviewed Guillaume Côté, a principal male dancer with the National Ballet of Canada. We chatted about being a boy and having to dress as a flower, or being a young man in your teens and having to wear tights and be a cat. He told me that boys should use these moments to work on their artistry.

"You feel silly to pretend you're a flower," he said. "But are you a happy flower or are you a sad flower? It's corny and I think that's where confidence comes in because you have to be confident enough to be corny or to fall into a feeling. Somebody's asking you to pretend to be a cat or something. You're just going, 'Wow, I'm a teenager. Jumping and turning speak to me but being a cat doesn't.'"

Côté said it was still important to try to feel your way into your character, even if it's embarrassing, because he believes that artistry is made of confidence and imagination, and playing an embarrassing role needs both. Based on my observations, famous dancers achieve their status in part because of their artistry.

"Once someone has lost imagination," Côté said, "I think it's very, very hard to regain it again."

Don't lose your imagination to an embarrassing costume. Embrace it: find your character and their reason for being, and dance your heart out.

Case in point: I've been hunting for that picture of me in the sprite costume, so I did what any Gen-Xer would do: I posted to my friends Facebook. No one had it, but one former dancemate of mine who's a few years younger replied that she remembered the costume and was jealous I got to wear it.

So whether you're a cat, four-leaf clover, flower, worm, or a sprite, there's a good chance someone out there thinks you're the coolest dancer on the stage. (And hey, there was an entire musical made of just cats!)

STAY IN TOUCH!

If you enjoyed the book, sign up for my monthly newsletter! I write it myself, so it's my words to you. You'll get the following:

- Sneak peeks at upcoming books
- Updates about online and in-person appearances
- Book and writing recommendations
- Recipes I love
- Contests
- And more!

Visit BetweenWorldsYA.com to sign up!

Prefer social media? All my links are listed under my bio, at the end of the book.

ACKNOWLEDGEMENTS

Thank you to Guillaume Côté of the National Ballet of Canada for allowing me to use a portion of our interview that first appeared in an issue of *just dance!* magazine.

The Donauschwaben Villages Helping Hands group has again provided me with answers to my questions about everyday life, including farming. I also frequently reference *Semlak*, compiled by Georg Schmidt and this time added to my research sources *Gara*, by Stefan Keiner. Trying to pinpoint exactly how the people of Semlak lived almost 100 years ago cannot be done: there were no smartphones to record every moment of every day. It means I have to use other sources to help me better understand what the lives of the farmers in Semlak *may have been* like at that time.

Growing up Catholic, I have had to learn about the Lutheran church and its teachings and practices. I've enjoyed my research. I'd like to thank Henry A. Fischer here for his help with better understanding confirmation as it's practised in this faith.

Understanding Sophie's rare disease can be difficult.

For this book, I attended a day of presentations held by the School of Optometry and Vision Science at the University of Waterloo, in Waterloo, Ontario, Canada. The presentations were for laypeople and they helped me better understand what goes on in the eyes of someone with macular degeneration.

Thank you to Michelle Fairbanks of Fresh Design for her help (and patience!) on the design for this cover. Conveying the lighter feel of this book while staying true to the series design proved more difficult than I had imagined.

I am always indebted to my editorial team, Heather Wright and Susan Fish (Storywell), for their input and honest feedback on my ideas and writing. This story wouldn't have come together as wonderfully as it has without their help.

Last, thank you to my family—Corey, Khristopher, and Jonnathan—for their support. I aimed to write and publish three novels this year, and I've done it! But it wouldn't have happened without their patience and love.

ABOUT LORI

Photo by Erin Watt Photography

Lori Wolf-Heffner is a former competitive dancer, dance teacher, and theatre manager. She was a member of the first Canadian National Tap Team, back in 1996, under the leadership of Bonnie Dyer, with choreographer Mathew Clark. She's written for *Dance Canada Quarterly*, *just dance!* magazine, and *The Dance Current* (all under Lori Straus).

Fluent in German, Lori lived in Germany for three years, never once realizing just how close she was to some of the villages her ancestors left to migrate to Eastern Europe in the 1700s.

Lori lives in Waterloo, Ontario, Canada, with her husband and two sons. She is a member of The Writers' Union of Canada and the Alliance of Independent Authors.

facebook.com/loriwolfheffner

x.com/LoriWolfHeffner

instagram.com/loriwolfheffner

goodreads.com/lori_wolf-heffner

bookbub.com/author/lori-wolf-heffner

pinterest.com/loriwolfheffner

amazon.com/author/loriwolfheffner